WITH THIS RING

TO HAVE AND TO HOLD DUET BOOK ONE

NATASHA KNIGHT

PROLOGUE

SCARLETT

Lace falls across my face. It's yellowed over the years and the smell that clings to it is musty. Old. But it's my mother's. The one she wore on her wedding day.

Baby's breath and discarded lilies litter the stone floor as the woman grumbles behind me. She's annoyed at having to work with the old veil when a brand new, prettier one sits unused in its box. I move my foot, crush the delicate baby's breath, impaling the fallen petal of a pale pink lily with my heel.

Funeral flowers for a wedding. An omen.

Not that I need one.

The stink of them turns my stomach. This isn't how I imagined my wedding day.

"Finished," the woman announces.

I stand, the petal sticking to my heel. I don't care. I look up to meet my reflection in the mirror.

"He won't like the veil," she says. She's a blur beside me.

I shift my gaze, letting my eyes focus on her. She's plump and short and has a wart on the side of her face with a thick black hair growing out of it. Don't judge a book by its cover has nothing on this one. She is as much a bitch inside as she looks on the outside.

"I guess he'll have to get over it."

"You should wear the one he sent."

I don't bother to answer her, although I agree. The veil was a gift from my brothers.

Gift.

No, not a gift.

Just another cruelty to make me wear my mother's veil for this sham wedding.

She snorts, turns to gather up the dress, the keys jangling on her belt. I could take them. Overpower her. That part would be easy. It's the men with the guns outside the door who'd be the problem.

Noisy footsteps on the hundred stairs announce the approach of soldiers to my tower room.

A tower. They locked me in a fucking tower. My own fucking brothers.

From the sound of things, they're expecting me to put up a fight. They'll take me kicking and screaming if I do. Besides, I know better than to waste my energy on them. I'll need it after. For the wedding night.

A man says something, another one laughs, just before I hear a loud crash, like something smashing hard against the wall.

It's then that it happens. Gunfire explodes just beyond my room. A bullet splinters its way through the thick wooden door and shatters the mirror, breaking my reflection into a thousand pieces, sending me backward into the stone wall.

The woman with the wart screams.

I right myself. Touching the back of my head with one hand, I somehow still manage to keep hold of the lilies. Suddenly, the door is kicked in, banging against the wall as heavily armed men in military fatigues raid my room. A cloud of smoke follows behind them, seeping into my circular tower.

They fan out, a dozen of them and I don't recognize a single one. These aren't my brothers' men.

The woman is on the floor blubbering something, sobbing.

I just stare at the door as another set of footsteps approach, quieter now. This one isn't in a hurry. And I know the instant he steps into my line of vision that he's in charge.

He's the one to worry about. The only one who's masked.

He stops just inside the room, surveys it, eyeing every soldier, every stone, every cobweb. And when deep blue eyes land on me, a weight drops in my belly, a hundred-pound cement block.

The woman with the keys stands, tripping over her words as she walks toward him. He looks down at her like he's irritated, and she doesn't get far. An echo of bullets shuts her down, splattering blood like paint on my neck, my face. The shots put her back on the floor.

Fuck.

I don't spare her a glance. I don't need to, to know she's dead.

The man's eyes return to mine. They narrow. And when he takes a step toward me, I take one back, knocking the chair behind me to the floor, panicking then. Animated then.

I turn to run but see a dozen sets of eyes staring back at me. The masked intruder, the biggest of them all, blocks the only exit. I can't even jump from the window. They're barred. Suicide was never an option, not for my brothers. They needed me.

But something's gone wrong.

And before I can decide what to do, before I can make up my mind to try to charge him, to risk bullets putting me down like they did the woman on the floor, he's got my wrist in his right hand and he's squeezing it.

My hand opens. Flowers scatter to the floor. I watch them, then watch him lift my hand to his face. His thumb comes to my ring finger where the hideous diamond catches the waning sun. For a moment I think he's going to break my finger. But he twists and forces it off. It's tight but he manages. He pockets the ring then shifts his gaze to mine again.

I swallow hard.

He cocks his head to the side, one hand still locked around my wrist. He spins me around.

I scream as he jerks me to him, his body a solid wall at my back.

He releases my wrist and bands his arm beneath my breasts. With the other, he pushes the veil off my neck, his hand rough against my skin, fingers digging, bruising. I think he's going to snap my neck. One quick twist is all it would take. He's a fucking giant.

But he doesn't.

Instead, the moment I turn my face up to his, he squeezes and instantly, my knees give out. My arms drop uselessly to my sides. He shifts his grip and as I slip, he lifts me up, hauling me over his shoulder, turning the room upside down before it goes black.

1

SCARLETT

I feel like I'm going to vomit. The smell is musty and damp, like an old basement. Cold is seeping into my body, making my muscles ache.

"Get up!"

Pain in my right side. I curl away from it, but it comes again. I groan.

"Fucking get the fuck up!" It's Diego. My brother. You'd think I'd know the feel of his boot by now.

"That's not going to help," another voice says.

Angel. My other brother. The slightly less insane one.

"There's no way out," he adds, voice oddly resigned.

"There's a window," Diego says before digging the toe of his boot into my ribs. "Up you fucking worthless piece of—"

"Leave her alone, you idiot."

I blink my eyes open, roll my head and stop instantly, the pain sharp at the back. I bring my hand up to touch the spot, feeling the bump as I try to remember.

Lilies and baby's breath on the floor. Shattered shards of the mirror crunching underfoot as I ran. Or thought about running before he grabbed me.

I look at my hand. The ring is gone. He pocketed it. I'm glad. My wedding day. My forced wedding. It never happened.

I push myself slowly up to a seated position. The musty smell, it's not only the room. It's the veil somehow still on my head.

The room spins and I close my eyes until the dizziness passes. When I open them again, a dark shadow looms over me. Leers down at me.

Diego.

"About fucking time."

I look past him to see Angel sitting across the room, his back against the far wall. Noah's head is on his lap.

"Hurry up, untie me," Diego says. He's been beaten. His lip is cut and there's blood and numerous bruises on his face. He crouches down with his back to me.

I see that Noah's hands are bound and Angel's must be too. They're behind him. I'm the only one they left unbound.

The white satin of my dress is smudged with dirt and blood, the hem black and the skirt ripped. I reach up to pull the lace off my head, the sound of hairpins dropping to the ground too delicate in this dungeon room. That's what this is. A cell in a dungeon. With three stone walls, the fourth a wall of bars. The window my brother mentioned is about the size of a shoebox and too high to reach. That's where the light is coming from. A too-bright square in the otherwise darkness. Daylight. I've been passed out since last night?

I wonder where we are. In the cellar of the compound where I was first imprisoned in the tower? I prefer the tower.

"What the fuck is wrong with you?" Diego barks, spittle landing on my face as he cranes his neck. I'm sure if his hands weren't tied, he'd have slapped me a dozen times by now.

I meet his dark, hateful eyes.

Without a word, I reach to untie him. Ever obedient. Christ. What the fuck is wrong with me?

I look over at Angel. He's younger than Diego by a year. He looks sad, and like I heard in his voice, resigned. He's also got bruises along his jaw and dried blood by his nose, but his face isn't as bad as Diego's.

"Is Noah okay?" I ask. Noah, our youngest brother, is still passed out.

"Yeah," Angel says, looking down at him.

"Not for long if you don't get these fucking ropes off me," Diego interjects.

I look at the knot, shift my gaze back to Angel.

"What's going on?" I ask.

"We were betrayed."

"Marcus?" My would-be husband?

He shakes his head.

"Lover-boy is gone," Diego tells me. "Ran away like the fucking coward he is."

"He's not my lover-boy. I hate him."

"Well, that makes two of us. Move." He gestures to the knot.

I'm about to focus my attention on it, when I hear the sound of a door clanging open nearby. Light falls into the space outside the cell. Heavy footsteps follow and I hear a man's voice. Another one that I recognize. One that makes my skin crawl.

"Fuck," Diego mutters, awkwardly getting to his feet as the men come into view.

Soldiers enter first, automatic weapons on their shoulders. Three of them, one carrying a heavy-duty flashlight. They insert a key into the lock and open the door of our cage just as my uncle comes into view. He's grinning like a fucking jackal.

His eyes fall on me first, skim over me. It would make my skin crawl if I wasn't so afraid. His gaze bounces off each of my brothers. He's clean-shaven, hair neatly combed back slick with gel. I can smell his signature overuse of cologne from here.

"Fucking traitor," Diego mutters and spits in his general direction. It doesn't touch him though.

My uncle looks at him, his lips turning down in disapproval. "Isn't that what we all are?"

More footsteps.

I look beyond my uncle as he steps aside. Two more soldiers, another man I know isn't a soldier just from the casual slant to his stance.

And then him. The one in charge. He's no longer masked but I know it's him. I'd recognize his eyes anywhere. I will never forget those eyes or the way they looked at me.

He stops just inside the cell, big frame taking up the whole of the entry, sucking up more than his share of oxygen.

My heart races at the sight of him.

The man I know isn't a soldier slides his hands into his pockets. He leans toward the one in charge and says something too low for me to hear. He's speaking Italian from what I can make out. I'd have known these weren't Cartel men anywhere. He's wearing a white button down and jeans. Casual beside the suited man who took my ring and somehow knocked me out.

The suited one scans the cell, taking in each of my brothers in turn and it takes all I have not to shrink away when his gaze fixes on me.

Instinctively, I touch neck as I take in his head of dark hair, the shadow of a beard. The scar along his right cheek does nothing to take away from his features. The opposite. He's dangerous, this man. Deadly. I'd know it even if I saw him out on a normal day in the normal world.

Not that I've ever lived a normal life in a normal world.

And even though I don't know who he is, my brothers do. I see it in their eyes. Feel it in the anxiety coming off them, their fear stinking up the room.

"Look who's risen from the dead," Diego starts, taking a step toward the man like the idiot he is.

The man's lip curls upward, and it takes the most minute gesture of his head to have a soldier on my brother, pushing him roughly to his knees.

The man's eyes shift to me again as if he's curious. He holds my gaze momentarily before scanning Angel and Noah, who is still passed out. What did they do to him?

"The boy," he says. They're the first words I hear from his mouth. His voice is deep and low. Quiet, but without a doubt, in control. I get the feeling he doesn't waste words.

A soldier moves toward Noah, boots loud, echoing. I wonder how vast the darkness beyond our little cell is. In the distance I see glimpses of light. Windows like the one in our cell, I guess.

"He's breathing," Angel tells the soldier when the man bends to check if Noah's alive, I'm guessing.

The soldier checks for himself, straightens and nods to the one in charge. He looks different out of his camo. Deadlier. His hair is a little wet. I guess he took the time to shower.

He nods to the soldier, shifts his gaze to me once more before turning to my uncle.

"Get it done," he tells him.

Jacob, my uncle, nods and reaches behind him to where he must have had his pistol all along.

"What's happening?" I cry out, a new panic taking hold of me even though guns aren't new to me. I live in a world of violence. It's my inheritance. It will be my legacy. I am the princess at the heart of it. Or I was when my father was alive. Since his murder I've become a pawn.

I pull my legs back, readying to stand. I'm barefoot, I realize. I must have lost my shoes in transit.

All the men turn to me.

I only look at the one in charge. He appears taller than before but that's because I'm still on the ground. He steps toward me. I scramble backward, my hand falling on the rusting metal frame of a cot. I pull myself up to stand, willing the nausea to subside. Willing my fear to.

I realize I still have my mother's veil in one hand. It's bloody too. Probably from the woman his men killed in the tower.

He stops when he's only a few feet from me. He's taller now than he appeared in the tower room. I've lost the four inches my shoes gave me. I have to crane my neck to look up at him and my gaze moves from his deep blue eyes, to the scar on his cheek, to his mouth, his neck. Another scar there. The edge of one. It disappears beneath the collar of his shirt.

This man has been through war.

"Kneel, Scarlett," my uncle calls out from behind him. "Show some fucking respect."

I shift my gaze from that scar on his neck back up to his eyes. Someone chuckles at my uncle's command.

The man's gaze skims my face, then down. I follow it, see how the blood had splattered over the torn bodice of my dress, too. I don't know why I'm surprised.

I reach to put my hand over it and cover myself.

"Do you know who I am?" he asks in the same quiet tone he used to tell his soldier to check on Noah.

My gaze snaps back up to his. I don't know him. I've never seen him before in my life. I study him, shift my gaze to the other one who's watching me, hands still in his pockets, but nothing. I shake my head.

"Grigori," he says.

Grigori?

That isn't right. They're dead. The whole family massacred.

I swallow, feeling the blood drain from my face. Because I know what we did to him. To them.

He smiles at that like he sees inside my head. Sees what I'm thinking.

"Say my name," he commands.

Grigori. That's their family name. My brothers attacked them after turning on my father.

"Say it."

I swallow, lick my lips.

He waits patiently. But if he's alive, he's had time to learn patience. It's been ten years.

Grigori. I do the math. He must be in his late twenties. I glance to the other one. See the resemblance. He's younger though.

"Grigori," I try out the name. "Cristiano Grigori."

I don't know how he hears me. My voice is barely above a whisper, but he gives the faintest smile and a slight bow of his head.

"Scarlett De La Cruz." His gaze shifts down to the swell of my breasts above the ruined gown. "All grown up. Shame you have to die."

My mouth goes dry. I'm speechless as he closes his hand over my shoulder, his grip slightly less painful than it was earlier as he forces me to my knees.

He leans down, brings his mouth to my ear.

I'm caught off guard by the tickle of the scruff on his jaw.

"Don't look," he warns, and I know what's coming. I know I'll have to look.

He walks away from me. I watch him from my place on the hard ground. He stands before my brothers as my uncle gives the order for Angel to be made to kneel beside Diego.

I can see their faces from here. See how when Cristiano crouches down in front of Diego, a dark patch blooms on the insides of Diego's trousers. My brother pisses himself. My all powerful, ruthless brother pisses himself.

I would laugh but it would be insane when we're all about to die.

Cristiano doesn't miss the expanding dark spot.

In my periphery I see Noah just starting to move. Will they kill him too? He's a kid.

"Where is Rinaldi?" Cristiano asks.

"How the fuck should I know? That mother fucker set us up. He's the one who orchestrated—"

"That's not what I asked you, is it? Do you know where he is?"

"Fuck no, you think I'd take the fall—"

"Then you're of no use to me," Cristiano says and straightens. He steps back and gives a nod. Just a nod. And my uncle points the gun between Diego's eyes and pulls the trigger. It's so fast, no hesitation, no time for Diego to beg. No time for me to even process, though I knew it was coming.

The sound reverberates off the walls. Why don't

they use a silencer? Blood and pieces of my brother's brains splatter across the wall, and my face.

I wince, wipe it away, but I don't scream. And I don't look away. I watch instead. Watch Diego as his body twitches, still kneeling as if not realizing he's dead, before finally dropping to the floor with a thud.

I don't feel a thing. Not an ounce of emotion.

We're all monsters, the De La Cruz family.

When I shift my gaze from my dead brother, I find Cristiano watching me, that curious expression on his face again.

Angel is looking at Diego motionless on the floor, half of Diego's head missing. He's next. He knows it. I know it. And he begins to whimper as Cristiano takes hold of his hair and forces him to look him in the eyes, while my uncle prepares the next shot.

"Where is he?" Cristiano asks. Same question.

Angel drags his gaze from Diego. He's shaking. My two brothers, both cowards when they're outgunned and outmanned.

I only wish it lasted longer. They deserve to suffer. Doesn't he know that? Doesn't he want that?

"Where. Is. Rinaldi?" Cristiano asks again. It'll be the last time he asks. I know it.

Angel glances sideways to Diego momentarily before shifting his gaze back to Cristiano, then to my uncle. He's trembling now. He used to laugh at me when I trembled.

"Please," he begs.

Cristiano releases him with a disgusted expression on his face and steps back. I guess he doesn't want to get his nice suit dirty. That alone is the signal my uncle needs to pull the trigger again, killing his other nephew. His godson, this one.

He's never been much of a family man, but I didn't realize he was a killer. Although I'm not surprised.

Cristiano's eyes fall on Noah who is sitting up now, looking dazed, shocked. His head is probably spinning like mine was, jarred awake to witness this scene. This massacre of what remains of his family.

"Bring the boy," Cristiano commands. Two soldiers move as if it would take them both to lift my fifteen-year-old tall but scrawny baby brother.

"No!" I'm on all fours then, scrambling toward Noah, the wedding dress slowing me down.

In my periphery I see my uncle raise his gun and aim at me. Then I see Cristiano's hand close over his forearm and point the gun down.

Would he have shot me? God. Would he have shot me, too?

I throw myself between Noah and the soldiers, spread my arms out Christ-like. "No!"

One comes to shove me out of the way, but Cristiano makes a sound. A tsk. The man stops, steps backward. They're like dogs, his soldiers. Well-trained dogs.

Cristiano moves toward me, my uncle on his heels.

"He's a boy!" I scream, pushing my back into Noah in my attempt to shield him.

"Boys grow up to become men."

"Please. He's only fifteen. He was five when it happened. Five."

My uncle cocks the gun, drawing all my attention.

"Look at me," Cristiano says.

I blink.

"Me. Look at *me*." He steps fully between my uncle and me, so I'm forced to. "How old were you?"

"What?"

"You. How old were you?"

I'm confused. I open my mouth, see my uncle's impatient face move into view beyond Cristiano's shoulder.

"Twelve," I say to Cristiano, forcing myself to block my uncle out.

"One of my brothers was twelve. The other eleven."

"We didn't...Noah and I..." I shake my head, panicked as I see Angel and Diego's bodies. Unable to block them out. "We weren't part of that."

"Hmm. But you would marry that Rinaldi bastard?"

"What?" It takes me a moment to process. "You think I had a choice?"

His response is a grunt but it's something.

"Did you notice the fucking door you broke down was locked? That I was *locked in*?"

"The boy," he says calmly to his solder, opposite my frantic tone. He holds my gaze as he speaks.

"No!" I'm on my feet and lunging for the soldier in the blink of an eye, fingers like claws, nails digging into flesh. But big hands grab me from behind and peel me off.

Cristiano turns me to face him and I get one good scratch down his face before he can stop me. He mutters a curse as he twists my arms behind my back, gripping both wrists in one hand. With the other, he fists a handful of hair half in-half out of the twist the woman had just painstakingly pinned my mother's veil into. He forces my head backward making me look up at him.

"Please. Not him," I plead, tears finally coming. "Please."

He studies me, eyes narrowing.

"He's a boy. Just a boy," I try.

"Like I said, boys grow up to become men."

He releases me and gestures to my uncle with a nod. My uncle moves. Noah's up on his feet, back pressed to the wall.

I drop to my knees at Cristiano's feet, hugging his

legs as he's half-turned away. "Please. God. Please don't kill him. Please!"

The gun is cocked. The echo is deafening. It's surreal what's happening and all I can think is, we're all going to die. He's going to kill us all.

But when I look up, I find Cristiano staring down at me with a look I can't quite name. Disbelief? Curiosity? Confusion?

I open my mouth to beg again. "I'll do anything. Anything you want. Just please—" my voice breaks.

My uncle mutters something, some sound of annoyance as he steps forward.

"Stop," Cristiano says.

I stare up at Cristiano.

He lays his hand on my head and I feel a glimmer of hope.

"Cristiano," my uncle starts after a moment of silence. I can hear irritation in his voice. "You need to kill them both. Like you said, boys grow to be men and she's a liability. Bear in mind, they didn't spare your mother."

I see from here how Cristiano's jaw clenches. How the hand at his side fists. He turns his head slowly toward my uncle.

"Maybe I should kill you too, then. Just to be sure." His words are a whisper. A hiss. The threat is unmistakable.

Someone chuckles. It's the casually dressed man. The sound is so out of place. When I look at him, he meets my eyes. Inside, I see hate. He hates me. Probably hates all of us.

I turn back to the two before me and see my uncle's throat work as he swallows. It dawns on me. He's afraid of Cristiano.

But hell, who wouldn't be?

Cristiano shifts his attention back to me and he does something strange. Unexpected. He rubs the bump on the back of my head like he's just noticing it.

When I stagger to my feet, he lets me. I go to my brother and take his hand.

My little brother is crying. My gentle brother. He was born into the wrong family. How Diego would have taunted him for his tears.

I look at Diego's body. See how that dark stain on his pants is bigger. He pissed himself in fear. And he got better than he deserved.

When I look back at Cristiano, he's watching me.

"Clean this up, Jacob," he tells my uncle then moves toward the exit. "Get them off my island."

Island? Where the fuck are we?

"I don't want their bodies on my land," Cristiano finishes.

He stops before exiting and turns to glance at me once more. Then, directs his attention to a soldier. "Put the boy under guard in another cell and bring the girl."

My uncle follows him to the door, grabs his arm

to stop him. "This isn't what we said. What we agreed."

Cristiano stops, looks down at where my uncle is touching him. Looks back at his face.

My uncle lowers his gaze, drops his hand and moves back.

Cristiano steps toward him, his body, his whole being a threat. "You do as I say. Period."

My uncle nods.

Cristiano turns his back on him.

"Bring the girl," he barks at the soldier and walks away.

2

CRISTIANO

Fucking Jacob De La Cruz is a piece of shit. A petty, opportunistic piece of shit.

The girl is arguing something, but I don't stop to listen. I don't care. They'll figure it out. She's safe, for now. So is the kid.

"Are you going soft, Brother?" Dante asks me.

I don't dignify the question with a response. He knows better. Or he should, at least.

I strip off my jacket, toss it aside when I walk into the main part of the house. I've only been back a few times since my return from the dead. Couldn't take a chance on being seen. Not before I interrupted that wedding.

Dust cloths are still strewn over most of the furniture and I stop to glance at the pieces that have been uncovered. At the paintings of my family. Another of my ancestors. The ancestors are easier to look at. I didn't know them. They don't mean much to me. But I move to the one of my mother. My father commissioned it when they got engaged. Or so I'm told.

I look up at her blue eyes. I inherited them but that's where the physical similarity ends.

Her blonde hair only one of my brothers and my sister inherited. They're all dead now apart from Dante.

The blood of the De La Cruz brothers crusts on my skin as I stare at the painting, undoing my tie, willing myself to remember.

Bear in mind, they didn't spare your mother.

And therein lies the problem. I don't remember. I don't remember a fucking thing. My own mother and looking at this painting she's a stranger to me.

"Is it done?" Charlie asks. He's talking to Dante. Dante is the reasonable one. I'm a fucking walking disaster.

"The girl and the kid are still alive," Dante mutters, obviously annoyed by the fact.

I force the anger I feel at not remembering down into my gut, to a place I can manage it. Barely. I move past the painting, through the living room toward the dining room. I stop between the pillars that hold up the vaulted ceiling.

"Are you okay?" Charlie asks when I don't speak.

Charlie Lombardi, an attorney with a penchant for uncovering details most want to keep hidden, was a friend to both of my parents and a man my father trusted.

I nod, take in the large windows, some still devoid of glass that let in the sun.

"Diego and Angel De La Cruz are dead," I say.

He studies me. I'm sure he wants to know why they're not all dead.

"Good," he says.

"You should have killed them all. Finished it," Dante says.

I turn to my younger brother. Just one year between us. Every time I look at him, I think how grateful I am that he's not dead. That he wasn't here when it happened.

"I'll finish it my way. In my time. This is up to me. Not you."

Dante snorts. "I'm going to get something to eat." He disappears into the kitchen.

Charlie gestures to the men working at the windows. "This project will be finished today, I'm told. You sure you want to be here?"

"It's where I belong."

The house has been in my family for generations. The bigger windows are an addition my father made at my mother's request. It was too dark for her otherwise. Even here, in southern Italy on her own island, she needed more sunlight.

My uncle told me that. Said she always hated the

dark. Got depressed in winter and on the rare rainy summer days.

And so, my father had the windows made bigger, but he fucked up. Sealed our fate. Gave his enemies an easy target because the bullet proof glass that was to be put in wasn't. Another betrayal.

I killed them too. The pigs who sold him that glass.

I will kill every mother fucker who betrayed us. Who had a hand in my family's massacre.

"We'll meet representatives from the families tomorrow. Everything is arranged," Charlie says.

"How did they take the news?" The news that the Grigori family wasn't wiped out as Marcus Rinaldi would have you believe. That they missed two sons. The ones who will avenge the murders of our family.

Charlie smiles wide. "They're thrilled the Cartel is out of the picture and that you've returned to take your rightful place," he says, the note of sarcasm in his tone subtle but unmistakable.

"I bet."

"We know the two who sided with Rinaldi. We still have the majority of support on our side."

I nod, walk toward the stairs. "They're either with me or against me. There will be no middle. Not this time."

He doesn't reply. But this is where my father went wrong. This is where he made the mistakes that cost my family their lives.

"I'm going to change. Are you staying for dinner?" I ask.

He checks his watch. "No, not tonight. I'm meeting with a few people."

"All right. I'll see you soon."

I head upstairs and walk into the master bedroom. It's one of the few rooms that's ready. I toss my tie aside, unbutton my shirt and tug it out of my slacks. I look down at it. Even on black, blood shows. Luckily it was never my favorite suit.

There's a knock on the door and I turn to watch a soldier manhandle the girl into the room.

Scarlett De Le Cruz.

Only daughter of Manuel De La Cruz.

Her uncle is right. I should kill her. But there's something about her that's got me curious and I can't quite put my finger on it.

I look her over. Even in the bloody, destroyed wedding dress, she's gorgeous. A fuck should take care of it. Sink my cock into her warm pussy and then I'll be over my curiosity. Be rid of her.

"Fucking brute," she mutters, stumbling when the soldier releases her. He did have a pretty firm grip but I'm sure it was because she asked for it. She seems like a woman who'd ask for it.

He looks at me, waits for my nod, then goes. He'll be outside. Not that I need him to manage her. I can handle Scarlett De La Cruz with one hand tied behind my back.

We study each other and for a moment, I see her on her knees at my feet again begging me to spare her brother. Not a word about herself.

She's out of breath from the haul up the stairs or from her fight with the soldier. Not very smart if she wasted her energy on that.

I continue to strip off my clothes, undoing my cuffs and two buttons on the front before pulling it off over my head. I follow her eyes as they take me in, her eyebrows knitting together momentarily, forehead wrinkling. Not sure if it's at that tattoos or the scars, but either way I stand there and let her have a good look. While she does, I do the same. I study her because there's something in those honey-colored eyes I don't understand. Something that goes against everything I have learned is true.

But fuck that shit.

Pretty girls are a dime a dozen. There's nothing special about this one. She makes my dick hard. That's all I have to worry about.

"Take off your dress," I tell her.

Her eyes narrow and she cocks her head to the side. She's petulant. A pain in the ass.

But a nagging voice tells me there's more than those things. It'd be simple if she were just those things. And I know exactly what it is. She's loyal. A trait not easily come by in my line of work. She humiliated herself, threw herself at my feet to save her brother.

It's too bad she's loyal to the wrong side.

"Are you hard of hearing?" I ask.

She just glares.

I gesture to the gown. "It's dirty. You're covered in blood and brains. Not to mention it's fucking ugly. I don't want you to dirty my things."

Her eyebrows rise on her forehead. "You don't want me to dirty your things?"

"Correct."

"I want my veil. Your goon wouldn't let me get my veil before he dragged me out of there."

I snort at that, take off my shoes and socks, undo my belt and pants. I turn and walk toward the bathroom, stopping at the door to look back at her momentarily.

"I thought you were forced to marry Rinaldi. Isn't that what you said? Or was it a lie to save your neck? So why in hell would you want any remembrance of the supposedly forced nuptials I interrupted."

Her gaze drops to the unzipped crotch of my pants and she's not quick enough to turn her head away as she clears her throat.

I was right. Just a dirty girl thinking dirty thoughts. Good. Dirty is good.

"It has nothing to do with him. The veil is my mother's." She stops, gives a shake of her head. "It *was* my mother's. And I want it back."

I watch her face. Watch her try to mask her

emotions. "She's been dead a long time. Why would it matter?"

"You don't forget people you love. Unless you're some kind of monster, of course."

Her words hit their mark.

I grit my teeth.

She doesn't know. She's just throwing words at me. Just words. She lost her mother weeks before I lost mine. Parents killed by those two assholes lying with half their faces blown off downstairs.

I turn into the bathroom and strip off the rest of my things, then switch on the shower and step under the flow.

"Hey!" She's at the door.

I look at her.

She glances down then quickly away as her neck and cheeks flush with embarrassment.

"I want my veil. I mean it."

"I haven't even decided how long you'll live yet, and you want a stupid veil from a wedding you were forced into?"

"I told you, it belonged to my mother."

"It's got your brothers' brains all over it. Ruined. Like the dress. Get it off and get in the shower." I switch off the water and step out, grabbing a towel to wipe my face, very aware how red her face has turned. "Please tell me you've seen a dick before."

"Fuck you."

I give her a smile I don't feel in my eyes. "I will. As soon as you've got that shit cleaned off you."

Her mouth falls open.

I wrap the towel around my hips and when I move toward her, she scurries back. Passing her, I walk into my closet, pull on briefs and choose another suit. I hear the bedroom door open then close. I'm sure that's Scarlett thinking she can just walk out of here. I chuckle as I step into the slacks and slide my arms into a button-down.

When I return to the bedroom, she's just walking back into it.

"You looked," I say, dropping the suit jacket over the back of a chair as I button up my shirt.

"What? I'm not looking at you." Her face gets that pink hue again as she folds her arms across her chest and makes a point of not looking at me for all of a second.

"I mean you watched your uncle kill your brothers. You knew what was coming and you watched."

Her eyes darken to a deep caramel and suddenly, I'm taken back. Caught off guard.

Burnt sugar. The smell from the kitchen. Mom standing over the pot, swirling it. Smiling. We're standing beside her, watching in awe as she makes caramel.

I give a shake of my head. The image is gone as quickly as it came—a split second of memory. It leaves a void in its place and has me wondering if it's truly a memory or something I was told.

Focus.

Scarlett grits her teeth, jaw tensing.

"Why did you look?" I ask.

"Is my brother going to be okay?"

"Why?"

"Because he's my brother."

I walk toward her, and she backs up until the backs of her legs hit my bed. I catch her before she falls onto it, straighten her, taking her jaw in my hand, putting my thumb over her lips. "You like playing games? I'd be careful playing them with me if I were you." I release her and turn to walk across the room. "Do not sit on any of my furniture until you get that dress off."

Opening a drawer, I look at the array of cufflinks. My dad's supposedly. Fuck. Again. Nothing. Not a god damned thing. The only thing I recognize is the engagement ring I tossed in here after taking it off Scarlett's finger.

I choose a pair of cufflinks at random, closing the drawer a little harder than I need to.

"Why did you look?" I ask again as I turn to her, slipping the links into their slots.

"Because they deserved what they got. Actually, they deserved worse. You were too easy on them."

"Hmm." I study her. See a hate in her eyes I find familiar. That's good. That's what I need to see.

"Why did you have my uncle do it?"

"Why did I have him kill them?"

She nods.

"A test of loyalty."

She snorts, rolls her eyes.

"He failed. But to be honest, he'd have failed either way. Kill your own blood and I know you're a traitor. Don't, and you're not loyal to me."

She's confused, her forehead wrinkling.

"The reaper stands at his door either way." A knock at the door interrupts us. "Yes."

The door opens and my uncle, David, peeks his head inside. When he sees the girl, I see a flicker of surprise in his eyes, but he's quick to catch himself. I'm sure he'd agree with Dante. I should have killed her and the boy, too.

"Ready?" he asks.

"Two minutes."

He glances at her again, nods to me and leaves, closing the door.

I turn back to Scarlett, look her over and close the space between us. I give her credit for not backing away.

"Get that dress off. Get showered."

"Can you just tell me if Noah's okay?"

"He's fine."

"Is he going to stay fine?"

"For now. Get showered. I'll have food sent up. You don't leave this room."

"Why? Why didn't you kill us?"

"Yet."

"What?"

"Why haven't I killed you *yet*. That's how you should ask that question."

She swallows, worry making her face go pale.

"You may be useful."

"What does that mean?"

"It means I'm going to need something to fuck when I'm back."

Shock registers on her face and her mouth opens into a perfect O. I give her a minute to process.

"I will not be fucking you," she finally says, tone a little quieter.

"Face down ass up is my preference. So I know my options. Be sure to be in position—"

She raises her arm to slap me. Instinct or stupidity. Jury's still out.

I catch her wrist. "You're an angry little thing, aren't you?"

"You can fuck yourself, Cristiano Grigori. I will not be fucking you."

I chuckle.

She raises her left arm to do what the right couldn't. I catch that wrist too, my opinion leaning toward stupidity rather than instinct.

"Don't think what I did for you was a kindness and don't ever think to strike me. If you get rough, I'll get rough and you've seen what I'm capable of."

"Giving the order to kill you mean?"

I squeeze her wrists, walking her back to the wall. "The only thing keeping your brother and you alive right now is the warm pussy between your legs. Once I'm done with it, all bets are off, so I'd try really hard to ingratiate myself if I were you." I lean in so the tip of my nose is touching the tip of hers. "I'll make this simple so you can follow. Do not fuck with me. Am I clear, Scarlett?"

She grits her teeth I assume to stop herself from opening her smartass mouth.

I press her wrists into the wall and squeeze. "I asked you if I'm fucking clear?"

She winces, eyes wide. What does she see in mine, I wonder? Rage. Fury. A monster.

I raise my eyebrows. "Do I need to dumb it down some more?"

"I'm not stupid and you're fucking crystal clear."

"I'm glad to hear it."

She calls me an asshole under her breath. Not stupid enough to say it to my face at least.

"What was that?" I ask, cocking my head to the side.

She keeps her lips sealed.

"Did you fucking say something, Scarlett?"

"No."

"Good."

I look down at her blood-crusted dress, shift her wrists into one of my hands and grip the bodice.

"What are you—"

The dress makes a glorious ripping sound, cutting her off. It exposes her bra, her flat belly. I shift my gaze back to hers. Her eyes have gone wide, mouth still open.

"Get it off. Shower." I release her wrists and walk to the door. "Alec." The guard turns to me. "Keep an eye on Ms. De La Cruz," I tell him, glancing at her. "She doesn't go out and nobody comes in."

She's wordlessly cursing me to hell and back. All I have to do is look at her to know. Her hands are tight fists holding the remnants of her dress together.

"If she does anything stupid, don't touch her. Punish her brother."

"No!" she calls out.

I walk out, then stop and turn back to her. "Remember what I said. Face down, ass up."

She loses what color remained on her face. Good. She'll heel. Because the tables have turned on the De La Cruz family and I decide whether she and her brother live or die.

3

SCARLETT

I stand at the wall and watch the door close. I don't breathe until it does. I don't move until his footsteps have receded and a full minute has passed.

Punish her brother.

Shit.

He could have threatened to throw me back into the cell. Could have threatened me bodily harm. But he's too clever for that. He knows I'll obey if he threatens Noah.

Face down, ass up.

I can't even begin to think about that part because what the hell just happened?

And the comment about no one coming in. Who would come in? My uncle? I'm an enemy to every single person in this house. I guess he wants to be sure I'm in one piece when he gets back to do what he thinks he's going to do.

I shake my head, try to clear that thought and the ones that follow. Because I'm not stupid. He doesn't need my permission to do anything.

I look down at myself, at the torn, ruined dress, then shift my gaze around the room. I thought maybe we were at Rinaldi's compound where he'd been keeping me the days leading up to the wedding. But I don't think that's right. I only saw that tower room, but this isn't the same place.

I'm in a large room. A master suite with what looks like a custom-made King-size bed against one wall and antique looking furniture, a desk, a dresser, and the nightstands. One door for the closet and another to the bathroom. The last one leads out into the hallway where I have no doubt Alec, the soldier, is still standing guard.

There are three windows along one wall. The other walls don't have windows.

He'd said island. He didn't want my brother's bodies on his island.

I walk to one of the windows and look outside, gasping at what I see because for miles and miles it's just blue. The view from the next window, and the one beside it, are the same. I open one, only to breathe in cold, salty air and listen to the sound of the ocean. Are we still in Italy? I was passed out overnight. He could have taken me anywhere.

Rinaldi's complex is just outside of Rome. We aren't anywhere near Rome.

Just then I hear a loud sound from overhead. I'm about to lean my head out to see what it is when the helicopter comes into view, turning sharply as it flies over the water and out of sight around the building.

A helicopter. An island. My brother downstairs in some cell.

Fuck.

Where the hell are we and how are we going to get out of here?

I close my eyes and force a deep breath in then out. I have to stay calm. I have to think.

Peering out the window, I look down and my belly flips. I hate heights and there's a good hundred-foot drop into the ocean. The house is built into the rocky cliff face of the island. This wouldn't be my way out even if my brother weren't locked in a cell below ground.

I close the window with a shudder and turn back into the room. When I move to rub my eyes, I get a look at my hands. I'm covered in dirt and blood and am suddenly very aware of the caked-on brains and blood on my skin. My face. My mouth.

Hurrying into the bathroom, I close the door behind me and brace myself to meet my reflection. Even though I think I'm ready for it, even though I've seen blood and gore and death before, this is different. And I'm in no way ready.

In my panic to get the dress off, I rip it the rest of the way, letting it pool around my legs where I'm standing. I do the same with my bra, panties and stockings, stepping over everything and into the shower.

The floor is still wet from Cristiano's shower. I have a flash of his naked body just then. Him asking me if I'd seen a dick before. I squeeze my eyes shut and tell my brain to banish the image. I can't think about that right now. And it's not hard to do when I open my eyes to watch pink water run down the drain.

Death. That's what that is. The deaths of three people, that woman and two of my brothers.

Condensation from his shower hasn't yet faded from the glass walls as I adjust the water as hot as I can stand it. I scrub my face, my hair, and my skin, trying to process what just happened. What I bore witness to.

My uncle executed my brothers on Cristiano Grigori's command. My own uncle.

No, that part isn't what's hard to process. It's shocking but I know what kind of man Jacob De La Cruz is. I've known since my twelfth birthday.

My stomach turns at the memory. That's the thing that almost makes me puke when seeing my brothers faces blown off didn't.

There's something seriously wrong with me. I'm not upset that my brothers are dead. The only thing we shared was the blood of our father and a mutual hate for each other.

Noah and I are from his second marriage to his one-time mistress. He set Diego and Angel's mother aside to marry my mother when she became pregnant with me. I'm a bastard. Can women be bastards?

I shake my head. Telling myself to focus.

Is that when my half-brothers decided to do it? To kill our father and my mother? To take over the cartel? But then they waited twelve years to do it? I don't think so. They were never that smart. Even though I believe their hate brewed in those twelve years since my birth, it wasn't them who came up with the plan to turn on our father. It was only with the Rinaldi family's help that they could have executed their plan so seamlessly. Which is why I was set to marry the heir to the Rinaldi mafia family. It would seal our union, the De La Cruz Cartel and the Rinaldi Mafia. They'd own Europe with the drugs my brothers could bring in. Not to mention the more lucrative flesh trade.

It makes me sick to think of it. Of how much suffering my brothers caused before their too easy deaths.

Cristiano's family stood in the way, though. No flesh trade. Their one rule.

But greed won out. Greed fueled by years of hate.

I thought the Grigori family was wiped out but

that's clearly not the case. I remember the other man in that cell. The casual one. Brothers. Two survivors. Have they been in hiding all this time?

After shampooing three times and scrubbing my skin raw, I switch off the water and look around. I locate a stack of towels on a shelf and reach out to grab one, twisting my hair into it. I take a second one to wrap around myself. I look down at the pile of the wedding dress and underthings. Blood even managed to get on my bra.

I step around them and walk back into the bedroom. Clothes. I need clothes. But the first thing I see in the bedroom is a tray of food on the table. My stomach growls at the sight. I don't remember the last time I ate. Days ago. I went on a hunger strike before the wedding. It was the only thing I could control.

Walking toward it, I see it's a sandwich with fresh mozzarella, tomatoes and basil on still-warm ciabatta. There's a small salad beside it and even a slice of chocolate cake. I pick up the bottle of water and drain half of it, wiping my mouth with the back of my hand before taking a bite of the sandwich. It's good. I shove another bite into my mouth, then another before forcing myself to set it down. If I eat too fast, I'll throw up. I make myself chew before swallowing as I walk into the closet.

Cristiano's closet smells nice. Like leather and man, a scent I'd picked up off him earlier. Something I hadn't registered I'd done. It's not an over-powering amount of it like my uncle likes to wear. Even smelling just a hint of Uncle's cologne has the effect of making me want to puke.

The closet is huge and lined with more suits than even my father owned. I marvel at how precisely everything is in its place. He or his house-keeper must be a little OCD.

In one of the drawers on the middle island I find a pair of gray sweats and a sweatshirt, the only things that I can come close to fitting into. I drop the towel and put the pants on. I have to roll the waist-band over three times and even then, I still have to fold up the legs. But they still keep sliding down so I choose one of his ties and use it like a belt around my waist. His actual belts will be too big. The sweat-shirt hits the middle of my thighs, but I'm very aware of not having anything on underneath.

While I'm here I search through the drawers to see if there's anything I can use as a weapon, if I need to.

I chuckle to myself at the thought.

If I need to.

I will need to. He's told me what he plans to do. Is that really the only reason my brother and I are alive? And is Noah truly alive? Or did he just say that to appease me? To ensure I wouldn't fight too hard when he lays his hands on me?

Shit.

No. I can't think about that. He's alive. I have to believe that.

I return to the bathroom and pull the towel off my head. Rummaging through his drawers I find a brush. I meet my reflection and peer closer, shifting my gaze to the right to see the bruise high on my cheekbone where the skin is cut. Probably happened on the floor of the cell. I'm surprised I'm not more badly hurt although my head aches.

Setting the brush down, I open the medicine cabinet and locate a bottle of Aspirin. I'm about to swallow some when I notice it's expired. By about ten years.

I look at the few other containers and notice they're all old too. Almost like no one has opened this cabinet in a decade. That seems strange. I close the door deciding against the expired aspirin and work the brush through my hair wondering about that oddity but not lingering overly long.

When I'm finished, I squeeze as much moisture as I can out of my hair and braid it. I hate having the length of it wet down my back. Twisting the braid, I tuck the end into itself to hold it in place and return to the bedroom. I eat the rest of the sandwich as I survey the space.

I wonder if Noah's had any food. He eats like a machine these days. Losing my appetite at the thought, I wipe my hands on the cloth napkin. I pick up the bottle of whiskey, only half-full, and turn it to read the label. A bittersweet memory momentarily overwhelms me. It's the same brand my father used to drink. I'd forgotten. Strange how you don't realize you've forgotten something until you're reminded of it again.

I don't want to forget my parents.

I open the bottle and sniff. For a moment, I'm transported back in time, back to my dad's study with its cloying cigar smoke and whiskey smell. I hated it back then. Curled my nose up at it. Now I'd give anything to be there again. To smell that smell. To see him laughing at me when I twist my face.

Closing the bottle, I set it aside before starting with the dresser closest to me.

I'm surprised Cristiano didn't place a guard inside the room with me. I know that probably means there isn't a weapon for me to find. He's not afraid of me looking through his things. He must know I will. I guess he's also not afraid I'll steal something. Where would I hide it? Especially if he's thinking he's getting laid when he gets back from wherever he went.

Did he take my uncle with him, I wonder? And how closely aligned are they? He asked each of my brothers if they knew where Rinaldi is. He meant my fiancé. Marcus Rinaldi's father has been in the hospital for the last two weeks. It's all been hush-hush, but my brothers were anxious to get the marriage sorted before he recovers. *If* he recovers.

I met Marcus's father on two occasions. He didn't seem like a bad guy. But next to Marcus, Satan might seem like pleasant company.

I keep looking through the drawers finding nothing. Just more clothes, briefs and socks like any normal person. He's not though.

The image of him standing there with his shirt off reappears before my eyes. I couldn't drag my eyes away. He's built powerfully and seeing him shirtless was more dangerous than I thought it could be. Dangerous because I wanted to look. Couldn't drag my gaze from all those scars and tattoos.

I'm not sure which he had more of, actually, but the one thing making me shudder were the few names I recognized inked on his chest. Many I didn't know but I saw Diego and Angel's names along with Marcus Rinaldi. Below theirs was Noah's name. Some had lines running through them. None I knew.

When I open the next drawer, I see something familiar. My engagement ring. It sits among neat rows of cuff links. There must be two dozen of them. And there, just tossed in, is the obnoxiously big five-carat ring.

I pick it up, looking at it. Not because I want it back but just to see it. To remember when it was forced on my finger. Marcus laughing, a fool, drunk as he fake proposed to me, almost breaking my finger when I spat in his face.

Angel and Diego pretending to be as drunk as he was. They laughed but I could see it wasn't real. They just stood by while I was stripped naked at Marcus's demand to get a look at the goods.

My brothers had allowed the stripping. The humiliation. But they'd saved me from having to fuck him at least. Probably afraid he wouldn't buy the cow if he got the milk for free.

I burn with embarrassment at the memory of it. My stomach turns at what my own brothers made me do.

I throw the ring back into the drawer and slam it shut. Cristiano can have it and everything it stands for. If it's Marcus Rinaldi he wants, I'll bring him his head on a silver platter if it will free Noah and me.

But I want something in exchange. I want my uncle's head on a matching platter. Would he give me that?

Cristiano's reasons are noble even if they endanger the one person I care about. He is avenging his family.

He just has no idea who he's aligned himself with.

4

CRISTIANO

I wonder if she felt anything at all watching her brothers executed. She barely flinched. It makes me wonder what they did to her to make her hate them.

I'm sitting in the boardroom along with my brother, two of the family attorneys, my uncle and two representatives from the charity to which I've made a sizeable donation. Charlie didn't accompany me to this meeting. This is the legitimate side of things. He's in charge of the other side.

One of the women is ogling me from across the table and I'm trying to avoid having to look at her. I'm only half-listening as I turn the diamond link on my cuff around and around.

"Cristiano," Uncle David starts. "Are you listening?" He smiles to the women and gestures for me to get my head out of my ass and pay attention. But I can't be fucking bothered.

"No, not really, Uncle." I get to my feet as he clears his throat, looking annoyed. "Why don't you and Dante handle this. Looks like you've got it all under control." I nod to those at the table and walk away.

He pushes his chair back. "Excuse us for a minute," he says, buttoning his jacket as he follows me out the door. "What the fuck, Cristiano?"

I stop. Turn.

Dante closes the conference room door and folds his arms across his chest.

"I have bigger fish to fry, Uncle. This is handled. Papers signed. They want to throw a fucking party in my honor? No thank you. Don't fucking waste my time."

"It's a fund raiser and if your names are on it, the survivors of the massacred mafia family who have risen from the dead, come home to make good, well, it's good for business. Good for everyone."

"What do we care? The donation bought what we needed. It's a fucking front anyway." The money won't be going to the charity itself. At least not most of it. It'll line the pocket of another greedy politician who will in turn be in my pocket.

"God damn it. Keep your voice down."

"Dante will go in my place." I hear my brother's

muttered curse. "I need to get back to the island." I take a step away.

He puts his hand on my arm. "Is it the girl?"

I look down at it, then at him. I take a step toward him. David is my father's half-brother. He's in his late forties and at six feet tall, about four inches shorter than me. He's a businessman. Built like he sits behind a desk all day.

And he's overstepping.

"I've got bigger priorities, Uncle. You handle this. This is what you want. You were never part of our father's business. Keep it that way."

"No, I opted for clean money."

"No, not clean. *Cleaned* so you can't see the blood."

He grits his teeth, jaw tightening. He shakes his head with a loud exhale. "That's what you think of me? After everything? That's Charlie Lombardi poisoning your mind against your own family."

"Christ."

I run a hand through my hair and walk to the window, looking out over the city. We have different goals, my uncle and me. I want revenge. I want anyone who had a hand in my family's massacre dead.

He wants to capitalize off that vengeance.

And he hates Charlie.

Dante comes to stand beside me. "Hey. You okay?"

I watch the pedestrians on the street. Tourists and locals going about their uncomplicated lives. I turn to Dante. I nod.

He pats my back as we both turn back to our uncle.

"I don't think that of you. And Charlie hasn't said a word about you to me," I say. "I know what you did for me. I know if it wasn't for you, I'd be six feet under with the rest of them."

He nods. "You know I miss them."

"I know. I'm closer than I've ever been to finishing this." I just need to find Marcus Rinaldi now. Plans to take care of his father are already in place, but honestly, I have a problem putting a pillow over the face of a dying man. Not out of the goodness of my heart. No. I just want to be sure he sees me. Sees my eyes as I smother the life out of him. I want him to know it's me.

"Go," Dante says. "I'll take care of this."

"You'll both attend the gala?"

"We'll both fucking attend the gala," Dante says, giving me a look. "If I have to go, you have to go."

"Fine."

"Good. All right." My uncle pats my back. "Dante and I had better get back in there."

"Are you coming back to the island tonight?" I ask him.

"No. I'll stay in the city. I've got a few things to

take care of. You'll be meeting with the families tomorrow?"

I nod but don't tell him more. Just as Charlie isn't involved in the legitimate side of things, I keep my uncle out of the criminal side.

"Are you going with him?" he asks Dante.

"Wouldn't miss it."

"Why don't you stay out of it, Dante. Let Cristiano—"

"Like I said, I wouldn't miss it," Dante says, cutting him off. We exchange a glance. My brother has my back and I've got his, even if we don't agree on everything.

"All right," my uncle says and takes a step but stops, wipes the corner of his mouth with his thumb and looks around before asking his question. "What's your plan with Jacob?"

"Don't ask me those questions. You know that. You're either in the family business or you're out of it."

He studies me for a long moment, then nods. "I don't trust him."

"You think I do?"

He chuckles, pats my back. "Just make sure it's not the girl that's turned your head. Fuck her and get rid of her. You owe them that."

Them. My family.

"I know what I have to do." That's the one thing he doesn't need to remind me of.

5

CRISTIANO

erberus, my German Shepherd, enthusiastically greets me when I enter the house. I smile, crouching down to pet him. He's been with me for two years. A loyal companion. Dante is spending the night in town. I can't blame him. I'm not a lot of fun these days and now that we're back in the land of the living, he's making up for lost time.

Servants have cleaned more of the house in my absence. More dust cloths removed, almost the whole of the downstairs looking lived-in now.

The house is huge. Well, it's a compound, a safe place. It should have been, at least, and it will be again now that I'm back. For all intents and purposes, the island is only accessible by sea or air. Guards are stationed in a watchtower. The building itself is six centuries old. A castle for a nobleman whose name I can't remember.

Another damn thing I can't remember.

My family purchased the house more than five-hundred years ago when the owner's family fell out of favor with the ruling party at the time. We've managed to hold onto it since, and the Grigori family has lived in it for all that time. Except, of course, for the brief decade after the massacre when it sat empty.

The Grigori family has been running things in southern Europe for all those years. We've lined the right pockets, made the right alliances. And we made the rules for all the crime families to obey. Ones they agreed to adhere to.

Well, agreed is a big word. That's one thing my father did wrong. You can't coerce true allegiance, I know that. You either have it or you don't and if you don't, you cut it out.

But when the new trade deals were negotiated, I was a kid. Barely ten years old. And it did work for seven years until the De La Cruz Cartel and the Rinaldi Mafia Family joined forces, rounded up supporters, and took us down.

"Cristiano," Lenore, the woman who manages the house and one of the few people left that I trust, says as she comes out of the kitchen.

I appreciate the interruption and smile, relaxing

a little. "Lenore, it smells wonderful." It makes me realize how hungry I am.

Cerberus goes to her to take whatever treat she has for him. He doesn't like many people so those he does seem to take a liking to, I remember.

"Thank you. It's good to be back in my kitchen." Lenore has been with our family since before I was born and is more like a grandmother than staff. While my mom loved baking, she wasn't always successful, and she couldn't cook a meal to save her life.

Crap. What a metaphor.

"You took lunch upstairs?"

"Yes, of course. And she ate every bite."

"Good. I have a request."

"You do?" I never have requests so she's surprised.

"My mother's crème caramel. Can you make it?" Burnt sugar. I want the memory back.

She appears confused momentarily but then nods, her smile a little sad. I know she loved my mom. "I'll start on it tonight and have it for you tomorrow."

"Thank you."

I turn to walk out of the dining room as a woman begins to set the table for one. I stop and turn to Lenore. "Two. Set it for two."

"Will David eat here?" she asks, her tone always

just a little different when she mentions my uncle. I wonder if she realizes it herself.

"No."

"Your brother?" Her eyebrows crawl up her forehead. Dante rarely spends evenings at the house.

I shake my head.

It takes her a moment as she figures out who I mean to eat with. She nods, and I walk out of the dining room leaving Cerberus to follow her to the kitchen where I'm sure she has more treats waiting. I don't stop to look at the portrait of my mother before climbing the stairs to my room where Alec is patiently standing guard.

"Anything?" I ask.

"Nothing. All quiet."

"Good."

I open the door not sure what to expect. Well, sure of one thing. It won't be Scarlett on her hands and knees with her face down and ass up. The thought makes me grin.

She'll make me bend her.

But I don't have a problem with that.

I ready myself for an attack but then again, I always ready myself for an attack. Like Alec said, though, all is quiet, and I'm surprised to find Scarlett is asleep on the armchair closest to the window, her head leaning against the wing.

I'm quiet as I make my way toward her. She's wearing my clothes which look ridiculous on her.

She has her feet tucked up under her. Her toes peek out from underneath and I see pink polish.

Her hair's in a braid that's coming undone, the shade even darker since it's damp. She has a book on her lap, thumb in the page.

I take it slowly, look at the cover as she stirs with a quiet moan.

She rubs her eyes with the back of her hand. There's a momentary pause when she opens them, confusion about where she is, I guess. After that, she starts with a gasp, pressing her back into the chair and looking up at me with those pale whiskey-colored eyes.

"You read Italian?" I ask, gesturing to the book.

She shifts her gaze to the book. Almost like she isn't sure what I'm talking about before shaking her head no.

"What time is it?" she asks.

"Dinnertime."

"Where's Noah?"

I shrug a shoulder. "Same place I left him."

"I want to see him."

I move to place the book on the nightstand, and she stands up, adjusting her clothes. My clothes. I look her over, only to realize one of my favorite ties is knotted at her waist. It's the only thing keeping the pants up.

"Hello? I want to see my brother. I did what you said. I showered and I haven't done *anything stupid*."

I smile at that and walk to the closet to change into a pair of jeans and a sweater. "But you also weren't waiting for me as I instructed."

"I'm not—"

"You don't make demands, Scarlett," I throw over my shoulder, noticing the drawer where my cufflinks are stored, isn't properly closed. It gets stuck sometimes, but I remember closing it.

Glancing at her, I go to it, open it.

"I didn't steal anything if that's what you're thinking."

No, she didn't. Not even the ring I took from her. "You looked through everything?" I ask, turning back to her.

"Yep."

"Good. That's out of your system then."

She just narrows her eyes at me. Suspicious of me. She should be.

I walk into the closet and when I emerge after changing, she's standing at the window looking outside.

"Where are we?"

"Isola San Nicola."

She folds her arms over her chest and shifts her weight onto her right foot. She's uncertain but trying not to show it.

"Where is Isola San Nicola exactly?"

"Off Porto Di Napoli."

"Naples?"

I nod. "I'm hungry."

"How did you get me here? Get my brothers here?"

"Chopper and boat." I walk to the door and open it. "Let's go."

"Where?"

"Dinner. I'm hungry."

"So you've said. I want to see my brother."

"I've also said you don't make demands, but I gather you have selective hearing. Now unless you want to get fucked before eating, get your ass out the door."

Her jaw tightens and she digs her heels in, eyes brightening with anger. "No. And I'm not fucking you."

I shake my head. "Fury."

"What?"

I walk toward her, take her arm. "The Furies. Greek mythology."

"What the hell does that have to do with anything? Let go."

I walk her toward the door. "Your face is the personification of fury," I say then gesture to my cheek where she scratched me pretty good before I stopped her. "Fury did this. Rage. Now, I'm hungry. We're going to eat."

She resists but isn't a match physically. "I thought you were just going to fuck me when you got back. Isn't that what you threatened?"

At that I stop, smiling a true smile. I look down at her, not releasing her as she struggles to peel my hand off.

"Is that what you were dreaming about?"

"What? No!"

I look her over, liking her in my clothes. Liking how small she is in them. I lean down, inhale when I'm close. She smells like me. My shampoo. My soap. "Don't worry, we'll get to the fucking," I whisper. When I pull back, I see her pulse thrumming in her neck, see how her face is flushed red.

"That's not what I meant."

"First, dinner." I drag her through the door. Alec watches, snorts like it's what he expected.

"I'm not eating with you. I want to see my brother and I want to go home!"

"And where exactly is home?"

At that, she falters. I decide not to waste time, so before she realizes what's happening, I bend down to lift her and toss her over my shoulder.

She yelps when I do. Then yelps once more when I smack her ass.

"Quiet," I tell her.

She doesn't quiet though. She doesn't seem like the quiet type. She struggles, hurtling curses at me as I carry her down the stairs, through the living room. I nod at the soldier standing nearby and enter the dining room where I plant her to sit.

"Does your mother know the language you use?"

"My mother doesn't know much these days since she's dead, asshole."

I stop, take in her anger. I drop it because why the fuck did I even say that? Her mother is dead. Murdered like mine. Well, maybe not exactly like mine.

Lenore, who opens the dining room door, quickly disappears back through it.

"I want to see my brother," Scarlett demands. I guess gaining a little backbone at my silence. "I'm not sitting here with you or eating with you. You killed my brothers. You've probably hurt Noah. You—"

I slam my hands on the arms of her chair and she jumps. I lean in close. I want to be sure I have her attention.

She leans away from me, quietly staring at me wide-eyed.

"I have not hurt your brother."

"How do I know that? I can't know it until I see him for myself."

"You know because I just told you."

She juts her chin out.

"You will sit with me and you will eat with me." She opens her mouth to argue but I continue. "And afterward, I'll consider letting you see your brother." My concession. Not that I need to make one.

Her expression changes and she searches my eyes. Probably trying to gauge if I mean it or not.

"Understand?" I ask.

"What does that mean? You'll consider it?"

"It means if you're good, I'll take you to him so you can see for yourself that he's fine."

She stops, studies me for a long minute. "Do you promise?" she asks, earnest and innocent.

I'm surprised at the question. It's almost childish. But I nod.

She stares up at me like she's not quite sure whether or not to believe me. But what choice does she have?

"Are we eating in peace?"

She nods. "Fine."

I straighten and when I turn to take my seat, I hear her mutter *Neanderthal* under her breath. I smile. Pretend I didn't hear it as the kitchen door opens and Cerberus enters ahead of Lenore.

6

SCARLETT

"Jesus!" I'm startled at the look of the very large and very excited German Shepherd that comes through the door.

Cristiano turns to look at me with a grin on his face—*asshole*—which is gone the instant the giant hound sniffs me then sets his head on my lap, tail wagging like we're old friends.

I admit, this is a scary looking dog but they're usually the sweetest. It's the little fuckers you have to watch for. I still remember a friend's yappy poodle chasing me around the dining room table on my first visit to her house when I was barely five.

"Well, hi there. What's your name, sweetie?" I ask him in a voice that makes Cristiano roll his eyes as I lean down to cuddle the dog.

Cristiano mutters something under his breath. I don't hear what it is, but he sounds annoyed. Good.

"Cerberus. Here." He points beside him, but Cerberus nuzzles his nose into my hair behind my ear. "Christ," he mutters and tugs the dog away. "Sit."

"Hey!"

The dog whines but sits, just barely, tail still wagging and eyes on me like he wants to play.

"Cerberus?" I ask Cristiano, feeling my eyebrows arch high as the food is laid out on the table. The feast includes roasted chicken, vegetables, potatoes and salad along with a basket of warm rolls.

"You know the name?" Cristiano asks looking surprised.

"I can read, you know." Arrogant fucker.

He harrumphs.

"You named your dog the guardian dog of the Underworld?"

He ignores me, pouring each of us a glass of wine. Then he places a hunk of chicken on my plate before pointing to the vegetable tray. "Which do you want?"

"It's pretentious, don't you think?"

"Which do you want?"

I look at the food, my stomach feeling empty again. "Everything."

He seems surprised but heaps food onto my plate before serving himself. I pick up my fork and knife but stop.

"Has Noah eaten?"

He picks up the chicken and bites into it confirming my earlier assessment. Neanderthal.

"I have no reason to starve your brother. Eat."

I do even though I'm not sure I believe him. One step at a time. When I see Noah, I'll ask him if he's eaten. If he hasn't, I'll figure out a way to convince Cristiano to give him food.

We don't talk for long minutes. I watch him from the corner of my eye. He eats like he's not used to eating in public or with company. And apparently, he doesn't feel any qualms about openly watching me as he does.

Cerberus comes to sit under the table, laying his head on my bare foot. He's soft and warm and I slip him a piece of chicken.

"Don't feed him," Cristiano says.

"Why? Are you afraid he'll like me more than he likes you?"

"I am his master. It's not about like."

I shrug a shoulder and abandon my knife and fork to pick up my chicken with my hands. He studies me, an eyebrow arching as I finish my dish then reach for the other drumstick. I give him a grin and take a huge bite. Maybe if I'm gross enough he'll realize he doesn't want to fuck me and let me go instead.

Not likely.

When he's finished, he wipes his mouth on his

napkin. He rises and leaves the table, disappearing into the kitchen without a word.

Cerberus sits up as soon as he's gone and rests his head on my lap again. I feed him the last of my chicken, worry creeping back in.

For all my bravado, I am afraid. I don't know what Cristiano wants or what he'll do to Noah or to me. The chances of this turning out well for either of us are pretty much nil.

When Cristiano returns wiping his hands on a towel, I school my features. I don't want him to see that I'm anxious. He holds the kitchen door open.

"Cerberus," he calls and gestures to the kitchen.

Cerberus disappears into the kitchen as Cristiano returns to the table. He eyes my dish.

"You eat a lot."

"I was on a hunger strike." And I have to admit, I may have overdone it tonight. I put my hand on my full belly.

"Why?" he asks.

"To protest my wedding."

"A hunger strike is ineffective unless your life holds some value. It only weakens you."

"Sometimes whether or not you eat is the only thing you have control over. I guess you wouldn't know anything about that since you're probably usually the one on the other side of things."

"You don't know anything about me." He

watches me for a long minute. "What did you hope to achieve?"

"Nothing, actually. I knew it wouldn't achieve anything. Wouldn't change anything. I know my brothers," I pause, remembering. "Knew them."

"Mm."

"I sat and I ate. Can I see Noah now?" I ask, taking care not to sound like I'm making a demand.

"Finish your wine." He finished his and two more glasses as we ate. I've only sipped mine.

I pick up my glass and drain it. He raises his eyebrows as I set my glass down and wipe my mouth with the back of my hand.

Cristiano shakes his head at my bad manners, stands and pulls my chair out. I find this strange because I didn't think he had any manners himself.

I stand and follow him to a bathroom. He holds the door open and switches on the light. It's beautiful inside, like the rest of what I've seen of the house. Italian style with elaborately painted walls, some with frescoes depicting scenes from Greek mythology. It all looks like it's been touched up recently. Even this tiny bathroom has a vaulted ceiling, similar to the rest of the first floor.

"You eat like an animal," he says. "Wash your hands."

"I only mimicked my host."

"If I'm your host you imply you're my guest."

I wash my hands and switch off the water before grabbing a towel and turning to him. "Your captive then. Is that better? Call a spade a spade, a devil a devil."

"You come from a family of devils."

He's right. I do. So, I don't answer. Instead, I follow him through the large, open living room with its elegant, Venetian style furnishings and glance at all of the paintings we pass. I notice his eyes linger on one in particular. A woman in her late twenties. She's beautiful.

"Who is that?"

"My mother," he says without turning around.

His mother.

She was executed with the rest of his family by my brothers. By the man I was to marry.

I shudder with a sudden chill. If he notices he doesn't say anything as we proceed into the decidedly cooler and darker corridor, the smell of must already present here. It's the one that leads to the cells. I remember being dragged up here.

I make a mental note that we've only passed one soldier inside the house.

"Hold on to the handrail," Cristiano tells me. He walks ahead of me like he can see in the dark.

"There aren't any lights?"

"No."

"Are you keeping Noah in the dark?"

He turns and I can just make out his eyes from the little bit of light coming from the house. "Better than six feet under, isn't it?"

I swallow. Yes, I guess it is.

I miss the next step, gasping as I stumble forward. Cristiano catches me, steadies me, then wraps my hand around the handrail, his hand covering mine entirely, the skin rough but the act gentle. He keeps it like that, holding mine for a moment too long and I still have to look up at him even though he's standing on the lower step.

"Hold on to the handrail," he repeats.

I nod, breaking eye contact.

We walk on. Once we take the next turn on the curving stone staircase, I see light. I don't wait for Cristiano to step aside or lead me to it, but rush there myself.

"Noah!" I close my hands around the bars and see my brother sitting on a cot eating the last of his meal. The source of the light, a flashlight beside him.

"Scarlett!" He rushes to me, hugs me through the bars. "How did you get away from him?"

"She didn't," Comes Cristiano's voice. He takes up space at my back, too close, making the hair on the nape of my neck stand on end.

Noah looks up at Cristiano who has a good six inches on him and about seventy-five pounds.

"You ate?" Cristiano asks as I look my brother

over. He doesn't seem to have any new bruises, no
broken bones that I can see.

"Yes, sir," Noah says.

I can tell Cristiano likes this. "Have you been
beaten?" he asks.

"What?" Noah asks.

"Beaten. Did anyone abuse you?"

"No. No, sir."

Cristiano nods and turns to me looking at me
with a 'told you so' expression on his smug face. But
then he takes my arm and turns me away.

"Hey." I try to claw his arm off.

He stops, looks back at me. "You saw your
brother. He's fed. He's unhurt. Let's go."

"That's not really fair."

"It's exactly what you asked for."

"But...no. That's not...I want to talk to him. Can
he come upstairs? He's harmless." I gesture to Noah
as if to make a point.

"Are you warm?" Cristiano asks Noah over my
head.

"I...guess." I forget how young he is. Just a kid.
So unlike Diego and Angel were. "I have a blanket."
He points to it as if he doesn't want to be any
trouble.

Cristiano turns back to me. "You'll visit tomorrow." He pulls me to the stairs.

"He's probably scared down here all alone."

"I think he's old enough to no longer be afraid of

the dark. Let's go. If you give me trouble, you won't see him again."

I go with him because I don't have much choice. "Does that mean we'll both be alive tomorrow?" I ask when we're upstairs.

He releases me, looks down at me. Sweeps his eyes over my—his—clothes. "I haven't decided. That's my favorite tie by the way."

I look down at the end of the tie hanging out from underneath the sweatshirt. "I wasn't going to put that dress back on and I wasn't going to walk around naked, so I didn't have much choice. If you give me a different tie you like less, I'll give this one back to you."

He reaches to pull the sweatshirt up and I grip his forearm. Not expecting it, I'm not sure what he's about to do. Not that I'd be able to stop him if he wanted to strip me naked right here. But he just fingers the knot.

"It's ruined."

"I'm sure it's not ruined, and I didn't know it was your favorite tie." I think of something then. "Are my brother's bodies still down there?"

"You care?" He meets my eyes.

"Not about them. I just...with Noah down there..."

"Don't coddle the boy." He walks back toward the dining room. "Were you involved in the business? I wouldn't think your father would have allowed it."

"My father didn't allow it," I start, following him into the dining room where our dinner plates have been cleared and dessert and coffee are laid out. It's something different than the chocolate cake I had earlier.

He gestures for me to sit, then grabs a bottle of whiskey from the side table before taking his seat. Same as upstairs, it's the brand my dad preferred.

He pours two fingers of whiskey and must think I want some, but I shake my head.

He leans back and drinks a sip, watching me.

"And my father wasn't in charge for the last ten years, remember," I add on.

I shift my gaze to the cake.

He gestures for me to go ahead.

"Can I take a piece to Noah? I'm not sure how much you fed—"

"Your brother is fine. Eat."

"Then I'm fine too."

He rolls his eyes. "Eat and I'll send a piece down to him." I'm confused by this but then he swallows what's left in his glass and focuses on pouring more.

"Aren't you going to eat any?"

He shakes his head. "Don't worry, it's not poisoned if that's what you're thinking."

I hadn't thought of that. Should I be thinking of that? No. If he wants me dead, he can do it much more easily than going to the trouble of baking me a poisoned cake. I help myself to dessert as he watches me.

"You're too skinny. I like a little more meat on my women."

"I'm not *your* woman. I'm not even a guest. I'm your captive, remember?"

"Don't want to break you in half when I fu—"

"Okay, that's enough," I start but when I look at him, he's got a grin on his face. "You're messing with me."

"You're easy to mess with."

Well, I can't argue that. I take things too literally, too much at face value. Always have. My parents would say it's because I have an innocent mind. I would swap out innocent for naïve if I'm being kind. Stupid if I'm not.

It's quiet as I take a few bites of the generously frosted cake, although I don't really want more. I'm just not sure I'm ready for what comes next.

"Why do you care so much about this brother when you don't seem to care about the others? They were executed before your eyes and you didn't flinch."

I struggle to swallow the mouthful of cake and set my fork down. I'm thinking about how to answer, wondering what he must think that I can watch my brothers killed without emotion. Hell, what does that make me?

"Noah's just a kid," I say.

"It's more than that."

"He's different than Diego and Angel were. He's softer. Not mean or cruel like them."

"You hated them."

It's not really a question so I don't answer.

"What did they do to you to make you hate them?"

"Well, for starters they killed my mom and dad." I try to hide any emotion, but I feel it in my words. I'm also sure it shows on my face.

He searches my eyes. "But what did they do *to you*?" he asks, leaning in closer. His eyes are so intense and as blue as that vast sea was this afternoon.

I turn to look over my shoulder at the painting of his mother on the far wall. Electric blue eyes. Like his. When I turn back to him, I see that his gaze has followed mine and there's something sad in it. Something broken.

"You have her eyes," I say before I can stop myself.

For the briefest of moments, I see surprise on his face. He's quick to school his features and shift the conversation away from himself. "Are you embarrassed to say?"

"I don't know what you're talking about."

"Yes, you do."

I shift my gaze slightly so I'm looking at his forehead, not into his eyes. He's too intense. Too focused.

"No." But I feel my skin get clammy. It's the truth. I'm not embarrassed. I am ashamed. There is a difference. A big one.

He narrows his eyes and studies me like he's considering whether or not to pursue this. There's nothing to pursue. He's not a friend. Not a confidante. He is my jailor. I will not tell him more.

"All right," he says like he's finished with it, but I get the feeling he's not.

"Your aspirin is expired." I want to change the subject.

"What?"

"It's ten years old."

"You looked through my medicine cabinet too?"

"I had a headache from banging my head on the wall when you broke into the tower to kidnap me." I'm making a point.

"Ah. The maid must have missed it." He's either missed the point or is ignoring it. "Do you need some now?"

"Would you give it to me?"

"Why not?"

I shake my head. "I'm fine."

It's quiet again for a long time before he finally pushes his chair back. "Alec," he calls out and the soldier who'd brought me upstairs earlier appears out of nowhere.

"Sir."

Cristiano stands. "Take Ms. De La Cruz upstairs," he says without warning.

I feel my face pale, the blood draining.

Alec nods, not quite looking at me but waiting for me to get up.

Cristiano turns to me again and he looks like a giant from where I'm seated. Without another word to me, he takes the bottle of whiskey and disappears down another corridor.

7

CRISTIANO

I don't look at my mother's portrait when I pass it, but turn the corner into a darker corridor. I make my way to my study thinking about what Scarlett said. That I have my mother's eyes. A strange comment to make, I think, especially from her.

Once inside, I close the door. The desk lamp is on. I set the whiskey bottle down, pull my sweater over my head, and sit before pouring another into a glass Lenore left on the desk. She worked for us before, too, and has been living with her family for the ten years since the massacre. She was one of the few people who knew Dante and I were alive.

I took three bullets during the attack. Two to my torso, one to my head. They'd mistaken me for a soldier or I'm sure I would be dead now. No execution style killing for me. But I did watch from my place on the bloody marble floor that mom loved so much. I remember how cold it felt, even in the July heat. How that small, inconsequential detail stood out.

My older brother and father were already injured when they brought them in. My mother had been seated in her favorite chair. I watched the tears slide down her face as her husband and sons were made to kneel in a line facing her. Michael, the heir to the throne. Luca and Gianni just kids, scared and trying hard not to cry. The soldier they had mistaken for me, my best friend Jonah. My sister Elizabeth they killed in her room. Lenore's granddaughter, Mara, is the one body we didn't recover.

My family must have thought I was already dead, and I guess I was. Bleeding out while Marcus Rinaldi, the leader, Angel and Diego De La Cruz and their army of soldiers stood in our house, desecrated it, bloodied our floors.

They killed Michael first. Bullet to the back of the head while my mother watched. While we all watched. Even injured, he was a threat.

I think, though, that it was a blessing for him given what followed.

Fuck.

I forgo the tumbler and bring the bottle to my lips, forcing down big gulps of burning liquid even though my throat has closed up. Even though it feels like I'm already choking as sweat coats my forehead.

Opening the drawer, I take out the machinery. I made it myself, my home tattooing kit of sorts. I'm not half bad when I'm not drunk. But my tattoos aren't meant to be pretty. They're meant to never let me forget what happened. Never forget those who betrayed us. Those who will be made to pay.

Not that I need a reminder for that. My memory is fine now. Intact from the moment I woke up after almost six years in a coma. I just can't remember anything before. Well, apart from that night.

I set the bottle down and take out the disinfecting wipes to clean the spot on my chest where the names Diego and Angel De La Cruz are written. My reaper's list. I will reap the lives of every single person named. I'm a little more than half-way through.

For a moment my mind wanders to what happens then. After I'm finished. I don't see a future after that, though. I've never even tried to imagine one. When the last name is crossed off, I'll be done with anything having to do with this life, this world.

Cleaning the space that will be tattooed and then cleaning the needle itself, I get to work, the little engine humming. I dip into the ink, wipe off the excess. I don't use a mirror. Probably should.

The names themselves my brother tattooed. I remember how he'd looked at me when I'd told him my idea about the list. How he'd seemed disturbed for a moment before he'd grinned and picked up the needle to get started.

I'd sat through it without a sound, without a word. Whiskey at hand, hate in my heart and vengeance on my mind. He tattooed the names my uncle provided. We'd never even heard of most of them, but he told us their stories night after night, patiently working. Patiently preparing me, our family's deadliest weapon. Because as the oldest surviving son, it was up to me to avenge their murders.

I think about Dante. About how he'd gone off the island at the last minute that night. How lucky he was to have been gone.

It was him who'd found me still alive the next morning. When every single person on the island lay in a pool of their own blood, I still breathed. Not a day goes by that I wish I'd been dead too.

My uncle had then taken us both into hiding. It's the one time he and Charlie worked together. He swore Lenore to secrecy.

I guess my uncle wasn't ever really a threat to the Rinaldi family since he wasn't a part of the business. The only reason he's still alive. Or maybe they just couldn't risk killing him. He was and still is very well connected politically. To take out a mafia family is one thing. You're almost doing a service. Two mafia families at war and toss in a Mexican Cartel too? Win-win-win.

But to kill a man like my uncle, a legitimate businessman—at least as far as the public was concerned—who rubs elbows with the elite of Europe's high society, well, that's something else altogether.

And so, I lived. Broken and damaged beyond repair in some ways, but alive. And Dante lived in a sort of coma too as he waited for me to wake. He was sixteen at the time of the incident and my uncle, rightfully so, wouldn't allow him to retaliate.

Even without my uncle egging me on, it's not only duty that drives me to avenge my family's murders. I want it. I want the blood of their killers on my hands. I want to watch their eyes as I steal from them what they stole from me.

Not that it will ever bring back my own family. Or even my memories of my family.

That's the worst part. This not remembering.

I'm not sure how long I'm in the study but by the time I finish and stand, the bottle is almost empty and my chest aches where I drew the lines. But my mind is on something else now. On the girl upstairs.

Fuck her and get rid of her.

I'm not committed to that last part yet though. Not sure why. Maybe it's her eyes. Looking at them gave me back a memory.

Burnt sugar. Crème caramel.

I know it's my imagination making me think I can smell it as I make my way through the dimly lit house up the stairs and to my room. Alec is standing guard. He's Lenore's nephew, and a soldier I trust.

"Did she give you any trouble?"

"Apart from asking me to let her see her brother again, no. She's been quiet as a mouse."

"Good. Check on the kid before you go to bed, will you? Take him what's left of the cake." I may not be very principled, but I always keep my promises.

"Sure thing."

I open the door to my bedroom to find the two lamps by the bed on and Scarlett standing at the window, looking out at the water. She's still wearing my things and doesn't turn right away, but I see how her body stiffens when she hears me.

How far would she go for her brother? I have a feeling she'd die for him if she thought it would save him.

"Did you fuck Marcus Rinaldi?" I ask. I don't know why she wouldn't have. She was his fiancée. It makes sense.

She turns around and I see a bottle of whiskey in her left hand. The one I keep up here. I don't comment but I am surprised. Although it seemed like she wanted some downstairs.

"It's really pretty here," she says and brings the bottle to her lips as she takes a step. She falters when she does but catches herself on the back of the chair. "Considering."

"What are you doing?"

She raises her eyebrows.

I gesture to the bottle.

"Preparing."

"Preparing?"

Her eyes fall to my chest. She points a finger at it, arm not quite steady. She's not quite steady on her feet.

"You're bleeding," she says.

I look down, wipe away the smear of blood.

She shifts her gaze up to mine and drinks another sip, dropping down on the edge of the bed like she can't stand anymore.

"Yep, preparing," she says, and I've almost forgotten that I asked. "I figure if I'm drunk enough, it won't hurt as much. Also, I just don't want to remember. So, if you don't mind," she says, holding up the same finger she used to point at me as if to say 'hold on'. She glugs down a couple more swallows that look almost painful from here. "I'm almost done."

"Wrong. You're done now," I say, closing my hand over the neck of the bottle.

She doesn't fight me when I take it. Mostly because I don't think she can. She's drunk about half a bottle and judging from the size of her, that's about half a bottle too much.

"Christ," I mutter, looking for the cork, finding it on the floor by the window. "Am I going to have to lock up the liquor?"

"Does that mean I'll be around long enough for you to have to do that?"

"Is that what you're afraid of?" I ask, corking the bottle and setting it on the table before turning to her.

Her face falls a little, her shoulders slumping forward. She rubs the heels of her hands over her eyes. But when she looks up at me, they're bright again like she has a new idea.

"Do you know the story of Jacob the Liar?" she slurs her words.

"You're drunk, Scarlett."

"First, he tricked his brother." There's that finger again, making some drunken point. "Then his father. Do you know it?"

"Yes, I know the story. What does that have to do with anything?"

"My uncle is a liar. Among other things. He can't help himself. It's in his name. You can't escape your name."

I step closer, narrow my eyes.

"Are you always so philosophical when you're drunk?"

"I'm not drunk."

"Besides, there's no such thing as destiny. We have free choice. People choose what they are."

"You mean *who* they are."

"I mean *what* they are."

She considers for a moment before standing and

coming up to me to push her finger into the middle of my chest.

"Do you know the man you have aligned yourself with, Cristiano Grigori? Do you have any idea what he is?"

One knee gives out and I catch her elbow to steady her. I open my mouth to tell her I know exactly what her uncle is, but she shifts her gaze, distracted by the little bit of red on her finger. She looks from her finger to the smear of blood on my chest, then at the tattoos, at the reddened skin. She peers closer, wipes her finger over the name of her brother. Then, she scratches her nails across the tattoos, across that raw skin.

"Fuck!" I grab her wrist. "Like I said, you're drunk."

She looks up at me. "Did you just do this? Is that what you were doing? Crossing off my brothers' names?"

I nod.

She shifts her gaze to some of the others. The dozen or so that also have lines running through them. The few that haven't yet met their fate. Then she does something completely unexpected. She lays her cheek on my chest, soft and warm, her hair tickling my chin. She slides it over the tattoos.

"What the hell are you doing?" I ask, releasing her wrist.

She draws back.

I see the smear of blood on her cheek and she looks as confused as I feel. But then she touches Noah's name. When she turns those burnt-sugar eyes up to mine, they're wet. She sighs deeply, backing up. I think she means to sit on the edge of the bed but miscalculates and slips off the sheets to end up on the floor.

I shake my head. "No more whiskey for you, Fury."

"We're going to die, aren't we?" she asks me, eyes wide when she turns them up to me. "What you're doing now, it's a game and when you're finished playing, you'll kill us. Or have my uncle do it." She makes a gun out of her hand, points at her own head and shoots. "Pow. Dead." She touches her cheek, smears tears into the blood. "He's just a kid, you know." She shrugs a shoulder then lays down on the floor at the foot of the bed and squints her eyes to look up at me.

"Some girls are fun when they drink," I say, crouching down to pick her up.

She turns her face to me. "Newsflash. I'm never fun."

"No, I'm getting that. You're a depressing drunk." I gather her in my arms.

She smacks my chest but it's like butterfly wings fluttering against me.

I smile. It's kind of cute. "Give Fury a little whiskey and she turns into a little kitten." I lift her up and carry her to the bed, draw the blankets back to lay her down.

"I'm not drunk and I'm not a little kitten." Her eyelids flutter closed hair splayed out around her. She's taken it out of the braid, and it's got some wave to it. A thick dark mass on the pristine white pillow.

I walk into the bathroom for a washcloth, running it under the tap to wet it before returning to the bedroom. She's in exactly the same position as I left her. I can't help but shake my head.

This is not how I expected tonight to go.

When I touch the cloth to her cheek, she startles, gasping, eyes blinking open, hands coming to capture my wrist. On guard. I get the feeling she's always on guard, like me.

"Relax. I'm just cleaning off the blood."

She studies my eyes, tilts her head a little and peers closer. "Your eyes are sad."

I don't say anything. What can I say? I just watch her, this confusing girl.

She reaches up to touch my temple, the scar there, a divot of missing skin.

"My brothers did this."

Again, I remain silent.

She shifts her gaze to my chest again, my arms, touching the scars there. The two more distinct ones are where the bullets penetrated my chest and side. I'm used to it, but I remember the shock I felt when

I'd first seen them and imagine her reaction must be somewhat similar.

When she looks back at me, she looks resigned. "No."

"No what?"

"I didn't fuck him. I've never fucked him, and I swear I'll throw myself out of a window if it ever comes to that."

"That why they put you in the tower? The bars on the windows?"

She smiles, eyes heavy-lidded. "I'm sleepy."

"Half a bottle of whiskey will do that to you." I walk back into the bathroom to drop the washcloth in the hamper. When I get back into the bedroom, she's rolled onto my side of the bed, her head resting on my pillow, hands tucked beneath her cheek.

I pull the sheets back and consider what to do about her clothes. I decide to undo the tie, which is pretty tightly knotted.

She makes a sound, her face contorting.

"Shh. Relax."

She does. Just a harmless little kitten now.

I push the sweatshirt up a little to get the knot undone, see a glimpse of smooth skin, her belly button. I look at her face. She's pretty. Very pretty.

And out cold.

It's what she wanted. To not remember me touching her. To not feel the pain.

Do I believe that she hasn't fucked Rinaldi? I get

the feeling if she did, it wasn't by choice. The thought makes me grit my teeth. Makes my blood run cold.

I draw the blanket back and climb in. I tug her closer, so she doesn't fall off the bed. At least I tell myself that's why. She rolls over, her back to me, ass against my dick which my dick registers as an invitation.

I groan, adjust myself and learn something about Scarlett De La Cruz a moment later.

She snores. It's a quiet little snore. Mostly. It makes me smile.

Nothing but a harmless little kitten.

But when she nuzzles against me again, I don't think about how cute the snore is or how warm she is or how good her ass feels against my dick because, fuck me, it's going to be long night.

8

SCARLETT

I wake to a violent pounding in my head. I groan, turn over, burying my face in the pillow, the unfamiliar feel of it—mine is softer.

And mine doesn't smell like him.

My eyelids fly open and bright sunlight makes my head hurt worse. Two days now that I wake with a headache. This one I did to myself.

Whiskey.

Too much of it.

It takes me a long minute to get up the courage to look behind me. But when I do, I find the bed empty and realize what that sound is. The shower.

He did sleep here, I realize. I still see the indentation from his head on the pillow and when I reach to touch it, it's still warm.

I wanted this, right? To be passed out when he touched me? So, I wouldn't remember it.

What do I remember? Not much.

Lifting the comforter, I peer underneath and am surprised to find I'm still wearing his clothes. The tie is gone, and the pants are down around my ankles, but I don't feel anything. I would feel it if he'd touched me. I've had sex before. I know how much it hurts.

No. That wasn't sex, I guess. That was me being fucked in every sense of the word.

Nausea at the memory almost makes me forget about my headache. I manage to shove it away though. I've gotten better at that but I'm still not quite there. Not to the point of not feeling anything when I remember. I wish I could forget it. Have the memories wiped clean.

So maybe Cristiano didn't fuck me while I was out.

I reach down and tentatively touch myself. It would be sticky or at least the blood would have crusted. Men leave a mess. But I feel nothing.

The bathroom door opens, snagging my attention.

"Morning," he says when he sees me.

I draw the covers up and sit up a little, scratching my head, trying to pat down my hair. I can be a pretty wild sleeper. I know what I look like first thing in the morning. And it's not pretty.

Not that I want to be pretty for him.

"How's your head?" he asks, adjusting the tuck of

the towel at his hips, drawing my eye to how low slung it is. To the V of his belly. The line of dark hair that goes from his navel to disappear beneath the towel.

My face heats up and I open my mouth to speak but find it's gone dry. I clear my throat. "It's fine." I really want to brush my teeth.

"I'm sure," he says with a grin and gestures to the nightstand. "That's not expired. And you'll want to drink all of that water."

I look over, see the container of aspirin and the big bottle of water. "Did you..." I stop.

He raises an eyebrow. "Did I what?" He opens a drawer at the dresser to take out a pair of briefs. He drops the towel.

"Can you at least warn me?" It takes me a split second to avert my gaze but it's too late. He sees.

He grins. "Too much for you, Little Kitten?"

Little Kitten.

Give Fury a little whiskey and she turns into a little kitten.

I make myself meet his gaze. "I've seen bigger and better," I lie.

"I doubt that." He chuckles and walks into the closet to return a moment later, zipping up a pair of slacks. "And I've just figured out how to tell when you're lying."

"Oh yeah?"

"Your voice gets higher."

"Fuck you."

"Well, that was the plan, but you passed out."

So, that confirms that we didn't fuck, right? I turn my attention to the aspirin, busying myself twisting the lid as I remember that my pants were around my ankles. "Why were my pants off then?"

"Probably because they're about five sizes too big. I took the tie you'd knotted around your middle off, but I didn't touch you otherwise."

"Oh."

He walks over, takes the bottle from me and twists the lid off easily. "Child lock."

"Ha-ha."

"By the way, you snore."

God, did I? How embarrassing. "Everyone snores," I say to deflect.

He disappears into the closet once again and this time when he returns, he's pulling on a shirt. I remember that part of the night. The muscle. The scars. Those tattoos.

The lines through my brother's names. Noah's name still line-less.

"Why is my name not on your list?"

"You're a woman. Barely."

"I'm twenty-two and that's sexist."

"You'd prefer me to add you to my reaper's list?"

"Reaper's list?"

"Grim reaper. I will steal the life of everyone

unfortunate enough to have their name inked on my skin."

"Well, in that case my brother doesn't belong there. He had no hand in the attack and you know it."

"I know no such thing. I have a meeting. You'll stay on the island." He tucks the shirt into his pants then wraps a tie around his neck.

"Are you going to cross another name off?"

He just gives me a quick grin.

"Where's my uncle? Is he here?" I ask.

"Jacob? Fuck no. After you've eaten, Lenore will make a plate of exactly the amount of food you eat for your brother and you can deliver it to him."

"Really?"

"Really."

"Wait. Why do you care how much I eat?"

"Because I don't want to break you in half when I—"

"You know what? Never mind. I get it. Can I visit with Noah or is it really just deliver his plate and leave?"

"Five minutes." He pulls on his jacket. "Do I need to put bars on the windows?"

"What?" But then I remember how I told him I'd rather throw myself out the window than have to fuck Marcus Rinaldi. "I don't know, is Marcus Rinaldi here?"

He chuckles. "Don't go snooping where you don't

belong. You can help Lenore in the kitchen if you get
bored and you'll stay indoors."

"What about clothes?"

He gestures to the chair where a dress is folded
over the back.

"Anything else?" he asks as he pulls his jacket on,
making it hard to look away from him as muscle
stretches the material.

I shake my head. What the hell is wrong
with me?

He comes over to me and I tug the blankets
higher. With a hand beneath my chin, he tilts my
face upward. "Tonight, we'll figure out if you'll be
useful to me."

"What does that mean?"

"It means you'd better be useful."

"You mean I'd better not pass out so you can feel
better about taking something that I don't give?" I
don't know why I say it because in my heart, I know
he won't do that. He would have already done it if he
were that kind of man.

He snorts, eyes growing darker looking like a
midnight sky. "Careful, Little Kitten."

"Don't call me that."

"Why not? It fits. I was wrong."

"What do you mean?"

"You're not Fury. You're just a harmless Little
Kitten."

I tug my face out of his grasp, but he grips it again, this time tighter.

"Let go of me. Don't ever touch me." I close my hands around his forearm which feels like a steel bar.

"Did I touch you last night?"

"You're hurting me."

"Or did I take care of you when you needed to be taken care of?" When I don't answer, he presses the back of my head against the headboard. At least it's soft. "Answer me."

"I don't need you—"

"Answer me. Did I hurt you? Did I take what I wanted with no regard for you?"

I stare up at him and he stares down at me.

But then he cocks his head to the side. "Or are you not sure? Can't you remember?"

"I thought I was wrong about you, Cristiano. I thought you were nice."

He laughs at that. At me. And I hear how naïve I sound, how ridiculous and stupid.

"I'm not nice, Little Kitten. I'm nowhere near nice." He studies me, softens his grip then runs his knuckles over the curve of my neck. He tickles my collarbone and I wonder if he can see how hard my heart is beating in my pulse. He lets his gaze fall to my mouth then back up. "Or are you disappointed that I didn't do it? Were you hoping to get fucked? Wanting it?"

"Fuck you." I try to move away but he captures my arm to stop me.

"I see how you look at me. Would it make you feel better about yourself if I took it?"

"That's not...Shut up!"

"Then you could say it wasn't your choice. That's how it was with your brothers, right? The wedding? Not your choice? Your little hunger strike all you could actually do instead of standing up for yourself, instead of fighting. You say you'd have thrown yourself out the window rather than fuck Rinaldi but maybe that's a lie."

I dig my nails into his skin. "Let go!"

"I'll let go when I'm ready to let go."

"I hate you!"

"Is it a lie? Tell me."

"Let me go!" I reach my hands to his face wanting to scratch him again, but he takes my wrists and flips me over onto my belly. He leans his weight over me, so I feel him at my back. Feel how much bigger he is than me. How much stronger.

"Don't fucking do that ever again."

"Let me go!"

"Tell me. Is it a lie?"

"Stop." I squirm beneath him.

"Or is it that you just don't hate him enough. And if that's the case, if you don't hate him enough, then you are my enemy, Scarlett De La Cruz."

"I'm not weak. I did the only thing I could. You

weren't there. You don't know what happened. What
—" my voice breaks. I turn my face into the bed. I
hate this. Hate that it all still makes me feel like this.
That it has so much power over me still.

He draws back and suddenly I'm spun over onto
my back. He studies me, watches my eyes, a momentary softening in his. But then it's gone and he's all
hard edges again. A high wall erected with bricks of
hate laid one on top of another.

"You'll apologize to me tonight. First thing. You
will get on your knees and you will apologize for
what you accused me of. Am I clear?"

"Or you'll make my brother pay? That's what
they did too, and it worked. Kept me in line. It's what
you're going to do too, isn't it? You're just like them."

His hand is around my throat in an instant.
Instinct kicks in and I claw at his forearm. He's too
strong though and if he squeezes any harder, I'm
dead.

"No, Little Kitten. I'm nothing like them," he says
through his teeth, eyes dark with rage. "And I'll
make *you* pay."

9

CRISTIANO

She's ruffled me. Gotten under my skin.

I'm distracted when I walk out of the room. I fist my hand, relax it. I swear I can still feel the pulse at her throat in my fist. I need to be careful. I need to check my rage. I may need her yet.

And I don't want to hurt her.

"Cristiano," Alec calls out. He has to do it a second time before I stop and turn. I didn't even see him outside the door. "Everything okay?"

"Fine. Stay with her. She can spend five minutes with her brother after she eats. Then I want her in that room unless she's in the kitchen with Lenore. She's not to go outside and you're not to leave her side, understand?"

He appears momentarily confused and I realize

how intense I sound but he schools his features and nods.

"Good." I look at my bedroom door behind which is my infuriating captive. I give a shake of my head to clear the assault of her words. I'm walking down the stairs but before I've even reached the bottom, I smell it. Burnt sugar.

I inhale deeply and when I look at my mother's portrait, I see it. A flash of memory. Us in the kitchen. All of us. Her four boys. Elizabeth wasn't born yet. *My brave little men*, she'd call us when we were young. We were always her brave little men.

And for a moment, for an instant, I hear her say those words in her soft voice. I swear I fucking hear it.

"Cristiano?"

I blink and it's gone. Gone like it never even happened.

"Are you all right?" Lenore is rushing to me and I realize how I must look.

I straighten, scrub my face, glance up at mom.

My brave little men.

Lenore is calling for Alec to hurry down. He's the only one she trusts, too.

"I'm fine. It's fine." I take a steadying breath. "Is it ready?" I ask eagerly.

She appears confused but then her face breaks into a warm smile. "No, not yet. It'll take another half hour to bake and it needs to cool. You can't have it for breakfast until tomorrow. Do you remember how your mother would let you boys eat dessert for breakfast?"

"Yeah," I say, wanting to remember. Wishing that if I say that I do, maybe I will. "I remember."

Her smile falters a little and I wonder again if she hears the lie. If she knows I can't remember, not the events themselves. And not my family.

"It's all right, dear. It's very painful, I know."

I clear my throat, steel myself. "The girl." My voice comes out hoarse. "Feed her, make sure she eats every meal. I'll be back late. Only when she eats does her brother eat."

"She's very young and the boy even younger."

"What does that have to do with anything?" I snap, and the look on her face makes me pause. I take another deep breath in, wondering what the fuck is wrong with me. "They're part of the De La Cruz Cartel. Blood of those who killed my family. *Our* family." Because Lenore is as close to family as one can be.

"I know. I know who they are. But they were children, Cristiano."

"Like Luca and Gianni were children. Like Elizabeth and Mara."

She steps back and looks down for a moment. "Come have breakfast."

"I'm late to meet Charlie."

"Better Charlie than David," she says with an edge to her tone.

"What is it? Why don't you like him? What is it with you two?"

"It's not that I don't like your uncle, of course. I just worry because you're different when you get back after time with him."

"Hm." I check my watch. "I have to go." I think of something then. "Do one more thing for me. Have someone change the lock on Elizabeth's room. Put it on the outside."

She understands why, I'm sure, but doesn't comment. Just nods.

"I'll see you tonight, Lenore."

"Be safe, Cristiano."

That's her standard goodbye whenever I leave the island.

I get my shoulder holster from the study and tuck my gun beneath my jacket. I head toward the front doors, two eight-foot steel reinforced doors. I'm not taking any chances. The pilot of the chopper is in close conversation with Antonio, the head of my security detail.

"Cristiano, you want us to ready the chopper? You didn't call down, but it'll just take a few minutes."

"No, I'm taking the boat today. Alone."

"That's not a good idea. Tensions are high. People are anxious," Antonio says.

"Then follow me with another boat. I don't care but I'm taking the boat. Alone."

For a moment I'm sure he's going to argue with me, but I walk out the door into the bright sunlight. It's late fall so even though the sun shines, it's a cool day. Good. It's just what I need to clear my head. Today is a big day.

10

CRISTIANO

By the time I dock the speedboat in Naples, I'm more focused.

I'm surprised when I see my uncle David is here to greet me. He's standing beside the first SUV, one hand in the pocket of his pants, the other around the phone he's got to his ear. He simply nods in greeting, expression serious.

Antonio and the soldiers who will accompany me dock beside my boat as I secure mine. I wonder what we look like, me ahead of the three, all of us in dark suits, dark sunglasses, heading to the row of waiting SUVs with their tinted windows.

Money, I guess. We look like money.

And trouble.

The Grigori family back to take its rightful place at the top. Except that we're not much of a family anymore. We're a two-man show.

"Uncle," I greet him. "I didn't expect to see you this morning."

He tucks his phone into his pocket and shakes my hand, glancing behind me. "You should take the chopper. It's safer."

"I'm fine. I needed the air. Why are you here?"

He studies me as he considers this. "I have two names."

I feel my jaw tense but nod.

"Tell me you did what I said," he says.

"Which part?"

"The girl. Is she out of your system?"

"She was never in my system," I lie.

"You didn't do it, did you? You didn't get rid of her."

"She'll warm my bed for another few days. Leave it. She's not your concern."

"She's a threat. Her family will want her back."

"Her family's dead. You mean the cartel will want her back. Maybe. Maybe not. And if they do, it could be to make her queen or to kill her. If it's to make her queen, then she's valuable. There are those who are loyal to her, to her family. We have to think farther down the road, Uncle. We can still use the cartel and if I have their princess, then I hold something of value."

"And her fiancé?"

I raise my eyebrows. "He's no longer her fiancé."

"Call him what you want. He can use her to

secure his position with the cartel. It's easier to be rid of her."

"And if he were to walk onto the island to take her, I'd have the opportunity of a lifetime. But we both know he's too much of a pussy to do that."

"He's not going to be walking onto the island, Cristiano," he says, dropping the subject of Scarlett. At least for now.

"What do you mean? Did you find him?"

He looks around, gestures to the SUV. "Get in. We'll talk on the way to my office. You won't be late to your meeting."

I do, and he follows. I look out of the bullet proof window, glance at the row of SUVs trailing us. My uncle doesn't like to take any chances with his life. It's funny to see how much he values it, in a way. He wants to live. He has a passion for life. Or a healthy fear of death. Two things in which we are on opposite ends of the spectrum.

"Here." He hands me a folder out of his briefcase. He's old-school. Leave no electronic trail. Ever. It's probably what's kept him out of prison.

I open the folder and the first thing I see is a grainy photo of the man who orchestrated my family's massacre.

The younger Marcus Rinaldi.

I flip through the photos, look at the vast, empty land around him. I look at the men in their pickup trucks, the porch of the house he's stepping into. The bigger house I recognize.

"He's in Mexico?"

My uncle nods. "Making an alliance between the De La Cruz Cartel, which he considers himself the head of since he is engaged to Scarlett—"

"He can consider himself the fucking king of England for all I care. It makes no difference to me. Like I said, he's no longer engaged to Scarlett. She told me she'd rather kill herself than fuck him."

"Well, that'll be news to him then."

"Go on. I recognize the De La Cruz house. But what's this one? With whom is he forging this alliance?"

"Felix Pérez. Jacob's son-in-law. He's back in the picture and has some support within the Cartel. I don't think he's very powerful yet but if they joined forces, it could damage us considering our situation with the other families."

"I'm about to resolve that situation." I close the folder. "And I have no intention of letting them damage us. Were these taken with a drone or do we have men there?"

"No men. Too dangerous. He's untouchable as long as he's on Mexican soil."

"No one is untouchable. Ever." I look straight ahead, my mind working.

"What about the old man. You can take care of him. Maybe it'll lure Marcus back."

"I already told you, we're not killing a man who is in a fucking coma. That's cowardice."

He studies me for a beat. "You can't go after him in Mexico, Cristiano. They'll kill you on sight."

I look over at him. Does he see how little I care about that? As long as I kill Marcus first, I don't care if I walk out of there or not. I just have to be the one to end that motherfucker's life before I die. That's all I care about. "You said you have names."

He nods, takes out another folder from inside his briefcase where I see stacks more.

"George and Stella Normandy."

"Not Italian names."

"No, but she's Italian. George is American. Married about thirty years ago. They're heavily invested in the flesh trade. They run a couple of clubs, for lack of a better word, where patrons pay top dollar for use of the product—"

"They're people, Uncle." Product. It bothers me that he calls the women that.

He pauses, looks irritated for a moment before continuing.

"As I was saying, patrons pay top dollar for use of the women. For anywhere from a single night to several years."

"Then I guess business has been bad lately." We intercepted the last shipment, and my men are still working on repatriating the girls and women to their countries, their families. It's harder than you'd think.

Some have been slaves for years. Some don't want to go back home out of shame. And some of them, well, their families don't want them back. Dirtied goods. As if being kidnapped and sold was their choice.

"You could say that."

"How did you find out about them?"

"You know I have my contacts."

"And you won't say."

"I can't."

"Fine." My uncle has a lot of contacts. We pull onto the street where his office is. "Anything else?"

He looks out the front window. "You should have what you need and the couple in question has been...contained."

I nod as we come to a stop in front of his building. "Have a good day, Uncle."

"Let's have dinner. We can talk about Rinaldi. Make a plan."

"Another night."

"Soon."

"Soon."

He opens the door and has one leg out but stops, turns back to me with a strange smile on his face. "Leave a mess Cristiano."

I study him. For not actually wanting to have his hands in the bloodier side of things, he's more macabre than I'd guess he'd be.

"Always do, Uncle."

11

CRISTIANO

Charlie and Dante are standing outside of the restaurant a little out of town talking.

They're both dressed impeccably in dark suits and looking, for all intents and purposes, like legitimate businessmen. Dante's twenty-six now. My one remaining brother. Our bond is strong, but he can be a pain in the ass, too. Although Charlie's the same age as my uncle David, he looks younger.

Five SUVs are parked in the lot and several soldiers are loitering by their vehicles.

I climb out, adjust my cuffs, very aware of the eyes on me.

"Everyone's here," Charlie says.

"How many soldiers?"

"About two dozen. No firepower inside."

I nod and turn to my brother. "Have a good

night?" I don't like the nights he spends off the island, but I understand.

"Okay. How about you?"

I snort.

He smirks. "What's the matter, Brother, don't tell me you didn't get any." He clucks his tongue.

"Fuck off."

He puts an arm over my shoulders and leans in close. "I can find you a girl who looks like the De La Cruz girl if that's your—"

"I said fuck off." I shove his arm off me.

"Getting laid might help you relax a little."

I grunt.

"Hey." Dante moves to stand in front of me. He adjusts the collar of my jacket then rests his hands on my shoulders. "You okay?"

Am I okay? No. I'm not okay. I don't remember the last time I was okay. But I nod. "We should get this done."

"You're not doing it alone, you know. I'm right there beside you. We take it back together. We destroy the motherfuckers who tried to destroy us *together*."

I study him, smile, mess up his hair. "Thanks for the pep talk but it's all good. Let's go."

He smiles. I know he's got my back and I've got his even if we don't agree on everything.

We walk into the building. For as bright as it is outside, it's dark inside. It's a dinner club, not a breakfast club, with dark walls and curtains, tinted windows and elegance all around.

"Gentlemen," I say, taking inventory.

Dante does the same, moving to stand at the opposite end of the room.

A single representative from each of the five families in Italy sits at the table. I haven't seen them in ten years. I tell myself that's why I don't recognize them. Not because of my missing memory.

"Cristiano," Matteo Gribaldi says, standing to shake my hand. I only know it's Matteo because I studied the photos, the histories.

"Matteo."

"It's good to see you. We'd thought...well, we'd believed the worst."

I smile but it's just a stretching of my lips. I feel nothing.

He resumes his seat and each of the others greets me in turn. These men have been working with Rinaldi in the ten years I've been gone. They've participated in and gotten richer off the one thing that was forbidden to them. They're greedy, all of them. But it's not their greed that bothers me. It's their duplicity and their weakness I despise. Because only after I attacked Rinaldi did they have a change of heart.

I take my seat at the head of the table, noting the soldiers standing around the room.

"You are here because you agreed many years

ago, some when your fathers were in command, to the rules my father set. The one activity we will not deal in. The Rinaldi family is finished. The De La Cruz Cartel has been dealt with. And now that I'm back, I resume my place at the head of this table." I pause. "My father made your fathers rich. My grandfather made your grandfathers rich. And we did it without trafficking in human flesh."

"Cristiano, Marcus was the cancer that ate his family from the inside out. Without your family to unite us, we became divided. We agreed to things we should not have agreed to. But we are not all as honorable as your father," one of the men says. It doesn't matter who. They'll parrot one another to save their lives.

"Honor killed my father," I say, shifting my gaze around the room. "I will avenge my family. You're here because you did not have a hand in the massacre. You're here because I believe we can return to the original pact. Am I correct to believe this?"

"Cristiano," one of the representatives, an older man with whom my family shares the most history starts. Lorenzo Ricci.

I raise my eyebrows.

"They killed my father, too, because he stood in their way." He stands dramatically. "The Ricci family is with you."

"Rinaldi is still alive. Both father and son," one of the others says.

"I have rendered them powerless."

"If the cartel chooses to work with Marcus—"

"They won't."

"How can you be sure?"

"I'm sure." I don't mention Scarlett or Noah. The less they know the better.

His eyebrows rise up.

"Are you with us?" I ask. I could give a fuck about anything else.

He nods.

"You've risen from the dead, Cristiano," another says. "I stand with you and your brother."

All eyes fall on the final two. They look around the room and together, they nod.

I stand, button my jacket. "I'm glad to see we're once again aligned. Gentlemen." They remain seated as I turn to the door, Dante flanking me.

"They'll turn on us in a heartbeat," Dante says when we're outside.

"I know. I don't trust them, but I've already made the example. They will obey me because I am mightier than them." Mightier than Rinaldi or any other family. The instant they see weakness, they will pounce. I have no doubt. Even those with the more impassioned pledges.

Not too long ago I found a letter my father had written to my mom. The letter itself had to have been thirty years old. It had been tucked inside the pages of a photo album. In it, he'd told her how he'd grown up with stories his mother had told that his family were descended from angels. He told her he knew better, even as a kid, but knew she needed for him and his brother to believe they were the good kind of angels.

He'd said in his letter that his family, and he in particular, was here to watch over the rest of this criminal underworld. Try to keep some control over it. To rein in the evil we do.

My mom didn't come from a mafia family and I get the feeling he was trying to reassure her, to win her over. He told her in that same letter he'd fallen in love with her the instant he'd seen her. She'd been working for my uncle at the time as one of his secretaries. She wasn't even Italian. I know he was supposed to have married the eldest Ricci daughter and I know the turmoil it caused within the families when he eloped with my mother instead.

Charlie told me how it cost our family, but my father was in love. And that was all there was to it.

It's a fairy tale.

And the task I have embarked on is a hellish tale.

What that letter left out was how the Grigori angels hated the humans they watched over. Just as I hate every one of the men at that table. Just as I hate myself.

12

SCARLETT

I'm sitting in the kitchen flipping through an old Italian cookbook, my hand absently petting Cerberus when I hear the sound of the chopper. I look at the clock. It's a little after nine at night.

Lenore, who has been sitting across from me making a shopping list, gets up and puts the espresso pot on the stove.

"He'll want coffee," she says to me.

Alec glances out the window. He's been my shadow today and if it wasn't for Lenore telling him I could walk out to the greenhouse to collect fresh vegetables, I'm pretty sure I'd have been locked up inside all day.

At least I got to see Noah. He told me that Alec had brought down the entirety of the cake last night.

I wonder if I should go up to my room. Well, his room. Will he really make me kneel to apologize to him? And if so, would he make me do it in front of Lenore? I feel my face burn just thinking about it.

But he does deserve an apology. I do know that. What I said, what I accused him of, it wasn't right especially knowing what I know. What my brothers allowed to happen to his mother.

"I'll go upstairs," I tell Lenore, just getting to my feet when the kitchen door opens, and Cristiano walks inside. I'm surprised because I guess I expected him to use the front door. This seems so domestic.

I take a moment to look him over. I can't help it. His hair is ruffled from wind, the tip of his nose red with cold, and the scent of whiskey lingers on the wind that blows in with him.

His eyes land on me and stay there even as Cerberus rushes to him.

"Where is your jacket?" Lenore asks him, going to close the door. The temperature was nice during the day in the sun, but it's cooled off a lot since.

Cristiano shifts his gaze to the cookbook on the table. Even though I'm standing, I'm still holding a page open. It's the one with the recipe for the Crème Caramel Lenore made. I had a taste, and it was amazing.

He finally turns to Lenore, giving me space to breathe again.

"It's fine. I'm fine."

I decide that's a good moment to slip away and take a step to the door.

"Scarlett." The way he says my name is nothing short of a command.

I stop but I don't turn back.

"Sit."

Lenore clears her throat and I hear her rustling around behind me.

"I said sit," Cristiano repeats when I don't move. "Get her a plate."

I turn around, not sure who he was instructing, but see Lenore set the Crème Caramel at the center of the table before producing two espresso cups, two dishes, and finally the pot.

"I'll take it from here," Cristiano says, and Lenore nods, unties her apron.

"Alec, you're dismissed too."

They exit the kitchen together, leaving us alone in the dimly lit room. Cristiano takes a few moments to pet Cerberus, giving him all his attention. It's strange to see him when he does it. How warm and relaxed his expression becomes.

Once he's finished, he tells Cerberus to go to his bed in the opposite corner of the kitchen. He then returns all his attention to me, eyes sharp as daggers on me.

I clear my throat and avert my gaze slightly, very aware of how hard my heart is beating.

"Dress fit okay?"

I nod, bite my lip.

"You have anything to say?"

Get it over with. Maybe he'll forget the part about kneeling. "I shouldn't have said what I said."

"Which was?"

"I shouldn't have accused you of...taking advantage of me."

"Of taking something you don't give," I say the words slowly. They've repeated in my mind all day.

"I'm sorry I—"

"Here. Say them here." He points to the floor beside him.

I draw a deep breath in, then out and in again. I'm not going to be able to do it. I just can't. Maybe it's that I know it's not Noah he'll punish but me, but I can't.

"Are you serious?" I ask him.

"As a gunshot to the head."

"That's in poor taste, don't you think?"

"I told you what I'd expect of you. You've had the whole day to come to terms with the fact."

"You want me to kneel. You want to see me degrade myself."

"Degrade is a big word but yes, I want you to kneel. I want to know that you understand your mistake. Your insult."

I'm on the verge of tears, I feel it, and I can't tell if they're angry tears or sad tears or I'm fucked and I'm going to have to kneel to this man tears, but they're just a few blinks away.

I push the chair back loudly and stand gripping the edge of the table for strength.

"I've told you I'm sorry and I mean it. I shouldn't have said it. But I won't kneel, Cristiano. I'll take whatever punishment you want to dish out, but I won't kneel. I swore it to myself with Marcus. With my brothers. And I won't kneel for you. Not of my own free will."

My heart is beating so fast I swear it's going to leap out of my chest. When he pushes his chair back and stands, instinct tells me to make a run for it even while reason tells me what a mistake that will be.

I whirl to run but he's on me before I've even reached the door. He's fast. So fast. And so much stronger than me. He spins me around, big hand in the middle of my chest pushing me against the wall.

I shove him, but he takes my wrists and drags them behind my back. With one hand he grips my wrists and winding the other one into my hair, he makes a fist of it, forcing my head back painfully.

"You won't kneel of your own free will? But that's what I want, Little Kitten," he says, words furious and menacing and spoken with precision. With control. He leans in close trapping me.

Danger. This man is dangerous.

"You're hurting me. Really hurting me."

"You think this hurts? How about this?" He squeezes the fist in my hair.

I cry out.

"Let me tell you about hurt. Let me tell you what happens to a woman who is made to watch her family forced to their knees before her eyes." As he says it, he forces me down, crouching with me as my knees hit cold, uneven tile.

"Please."

"Hurt is when her husband is humiliated before her eyes. When her first-born is bound, immobile, and executed with a bullet to the back of his head. Hurt is when his blood splatters across her face and the terrified screams of her children begin. Hurt is when we are made to watch my mother—"

His voice breaks and he has to look away, to swallow hard. When he returns his attention to me, the fist in my hair tugs even harder.

"Hurt is when your mother is stripped and *what she doesn't give is taken from* her before your eyes by *your* fucking fiancé," he jams his finger into the middle of my chest but at least he releases my wrists. "While your brothers stood by with guns at the backs of two children's heads to force them to watch when they turned away. To force them to bear witness to the unspeakable assault on their mother. That's fucking degradation, Scarlett. That's true degradation. So, don't you dare use that word. You have no right to it. You have no idea what it means to be degraded."

I'm sobbing now, not for myself, not because he's hurting me but for her and for him and for all of them. For my parents and for Noah, too.

"I'm sorry," I blubber. "I'm so sorry that happened—"

"That didn't just *happen*," he spits. "Don't you get it? They did it. They *made* it happen. Your brothers. Your fiancé." He shakes his head then, abruptly releasing his hold on my hair and stepping backward so I fall forward onto my hands.

He turns away, walking to the sink.

I watch from my place on the floor as he turns on the tap and washes his face, mutters a curse into the towel he uses to dry himself.

Cerberus whines from the corner.

"I'm sorry," I say again. "I'm sorry I said those things to you when I knew you hadn't touched me. I'm sorry that my brothers hurt your family like they did. I'm so sorry that it was my family who did that to yours. I'm sorry..." I trail off, sitting back on my heels, thinking, blubbering now because I am sorry. I'm sorry for all of it.

I rub my face, look up to find him watching me.

"I understand if you need to hurt me. Punish me for what happened. I do. And if you'll let my brother go—"

"We're back to your brother again. You'll do

anything for your brother." He runs a hand through his hair. "Thing is that my family's gone. Nothing will ever bring them back. Not hurting you or him or crossing off every god damned name inked into my skin. Nothing."

"I don't know what you want. I don't understand what I'm supposed to do." I wipe my eyes but the tears keep falling.

He comes at me fast and I scramble back but hit the wall. He takes me by my arms and hauls me to stand. He takes my wrists when I push against his chest, raising them over my head, pinning them there.

That's when I notice the red on his collar, the dried blood on his neck. That's when I realize what he's been out doing.

When I look up at his eyes again, I find them on my mouth.

"You'll cross off another name tonight, won't you?" I ask, my voice small.

His gaze slides to mine, then down to my mouth again. I lick my lips.

"Burnt sugar," he says instead of answering me.

"What?" Thick lashes cast shadows over his eyes, shielding them from me.

"Your eyes. They remind me of it."

I just stare up at him, unsure what to do, what I'm supposed to say or do or even think. He's not making any sense. He touches my cheek with his free hand, brushes fingers lightly, softly over my cheekbone, down to my jawline, over my throat and down. Down to close one hand over my breast.

I gasp.

He swallows as his hand weighs my breast.

"Are you afraid of me?" he asks more quietly but no more gently.

I stare at him.

"Not for Noah but for yourself. Are you afraid of me?"

"Yes."

He leans in close, inhales deeply. "Good. Because you should be," he says, his lips brushing my cheek, the corner of my mouth when he does. "Because you don't know what I want to do to you." He slides his hand over my belly and down.

"Cristiano," I say, his name a gasp as his hand travels farther south.

"Do you know?" he asks again and when he cups my sex over the dress, I rise higher on tiptoe. I wasn't even aware I was on tiptoe. "There's an emptiness inside me. A hunger," he starts, and I whimper, my hands fisted, wrists caught in one of his hands. His eyes appear almost black now. "And I want. God. How I want." Both of his hands tighten for one moment before he abruptly, unexpectedly releases me.

He steps back.

It's so sudden that I stumble forward.

He stares at me, all dark eyes and damage and barely controlled beast. "Sit down, Scarlett," he growls.

I keep my eyes on him as I reach for the back of my chair and lower myself into it trying to figure out what just happened. What is happening.

He gets the whiskey. He must keep bottles everywhere. He carries it to the table along with two water glasses. Too plain for whiskey, I think. My father would never have done that. For him, whiskey was a ceremony.

Without asking, he pours two fingers into each glass, pushing one toward me before swallowing the contents of his and refilling it. I don't touch mine. He then takes his spoon and reaches into the Crème Caramel sitting beautifully at the center of the table, the deep golden caramel dripping down the sides of the custard.

He doesn't cut off a piece and put it on his plate. This whole thing, us sitting here eating dessert after what just happened, it's insane. It makes no sense. But he dips his spoon in, slicing into the custard. As caramel drips off the spoon and onto the table, he brings it to his mouth and closes his eyes. I watch him. Watch him eat like he's just placed Holy Communion on his tongue. Like it's sacred.

When he opens his eyes again, he looks at me, but I can't read him. He eats another, bigger bite, then another. He gorges himself on it, drops of caramel dotting his chin.

"Eat," he says in that grunting tone.

I lift my spoon and with a trembling hand I take the tiniest spoonful. My throat has closed up. I won't be able to swallow it but I'm too afraid not to try.

"My mom used to make this and let us have it for breakfast," he says. I swear if someone walked in here, they'd think this was the most normal situation. Think he wasn't unhinged like I know he is.

He wipes the caramel off his chin, pours more of the whiskey into his glass and drinks it like water. Leaning back in his seat, he sets the cup down loudly.

"Eat," he barks.

I take another small bite, but he shakes his head and sits up. He scoops a spoonful of it using his spoon and brings it to my mouth.

"Eat it."

I open because I don't know what else to do. Before I've even finished that bite, he makes me eat another and another until I feel like I'll choke. When he finally stops, I wipe the back of my hand over sticky lips. I watch him stand as I force down the last of it.

I stand too if only to put space between us.

He backs me against the wall again and splays one big hand across my belly. Before I can think or open my mouth to ask what he's thinking, what he's doing, he kisses me. With sticky caramel lips, he kisses me.

Our eyes are open at first but then his close. When he draws back, he looks like he did when he ate his first bite of the too-sweet dessert. Like this is sacred.

He opens his eyes, kissing me again, sucking upper and lower lip into his mouth in turn. His mouth is warm, his taste sugary with a shock of whiskey. I feel him against my belly, feel his hardness. His hand slides up and closes over my throat. He's not hurting though. Not squeezing.

The kiss deepens, sensual and erotic, and I taste his tongue now. And something inside me wants this. Wants him. I don't know what it is or why. There's a part of me that's like the part he just showed me. Deeply damaged. Broken. So broken it can't ever be fixed. Can't ever be whole.

And when he draws back my heart flutters, missing a beat. I find myself leaning toward him, feeling the loss of him.

We look at each other for a long moment. I hear how quiet the house is. How completely silent. Even the sea outside, the walls are so thick in here, you can't hear it.

His eyes fall on his hand at my throat. He caresses it and I wonder if he's thinking about snapping it. Wondering if this would just be easier if he did snap my neck. I'm sure he can do it in an instant.

But then he drops his forehead to mine, and I realize his breathing is as short and choppy as mine. He mutters something I can't understand, then straightens, draws his hand back down to my stomach.

I look at it too, see how big it is. How it spans the whole of my belly.

"Did you know that part?" he asks, voice quiet. "Know what he'd done to my mother?"

I don't want to answer.

"Did you?"

I swallow. "I overheard my brothers after. I don't think they knew he'd do that, but they...they didn't stop him."

He looks at me. "Do you know what he said to her when he finished? Just before he slit her throat? Did they say?" he asks, eyes so earnest that it's almost sad to see him like this.

I swallow, shake my head no. I wish I knew, though. I wish I could tell him.

"I need to know what he said, Scarlett. What Rinaldi said."

"What difference does it make?"

He takes a step back, eyes shielded again. "I need to know." With a deep breath in he runs a hand through his hair then looks at me again. "Go to bed, Scarlett," he says quietly, like all the energy has bled from him. Like he has nothing left.

"How did you survive? How did your brother?

They thought they killed you all." They celebrated it. I won't tell him that part though.

"Dante was off the island. A last-minute change of plans. Me? They mistook me for a soldier. Executed my best friend in my place. I was in the room though. Bleeding out from the bullet wounds. Dante found me the next morning. My uncle and Charlie hid us."

I nod.

"Now go to bed."

"What about you?"

His eyes are distant, unfocused at least for a moment. "You want me to bed you?"

I feel my stomach do a flip but shake my head because that's the only right answer.

"Didn't think so. Go upstairs now then. The door across from mine with the lock on the outside, you'll sleep there tonight."

I look at him, confused. "Why haven't you put me in a cell with my brother?"

"I should. I would if I were smart."

He moves to the kitchen door, opens it. But when I stand there, he returns to me, comes so close I feel his chest against my chest and my back presses to the wall. He puts one arm up on the wall between me and the door. He's so close I can feel his breath on me, feel his heat on me.

"You need to go. Now. If you stay, I'll do more than kiss you."

I swallow.

"You have exactly three seconds to decide."

He gestures to the door with a nod of his head and I don't wait. I slip underneath his arm and scurry upstairs.

13

CRISTIANO

I let her go. Let her slip away. I don't know how I have the self-control to do it.

That night, I don't even trust myself to sleep in my own bed. Not with her in the room across from mine.

There's something about Scarlett. It's true what I said. There's an emptiness inside me. A hunger I need to fill. I want to fill it with her.

In the morning I take a shower in the bathroom in my office. I jerk off but it doesn't take the edge off. I want her. I need her.

Fuck.

I sit behind my desk and am running my hand through my hair trying to figure out what the fuck is wrong with me when Lenore knocks then opens the door to my office.

"Did you sleep at all?" she asks me, setting the

tray down and arranging a pot of espresso, a cup and a plate of food I won't touch. She glances at the photos strewn across my desk, careful to set the things down around them. She doesn't comment on any of it.

"I'll sleep tonight."

"Dante just got in. He's having a shower and will be down soon."

I nod. I have to remember Dante can take care of himself. He has a hard time being in the house. Harder than me. I know that. I understand it.

"Is Scarlett down yet?"

She shakes her head. "Go get her. Bring her in here."

"You could be less heavy-handed with her. You scare the girl."

I look up from the desk. "Well, maybe that's a good thing."

"Cristiano—"

"Get me the girl, Lenore."

She looks like she has more to say but purses her lips, nods and leaves.

Scarlett asked me last night why I haven't put her in a cell, and I don't know why. I don't know what it is about her. I'm not sure what happened last night. How things went so off the rails. Maybe it was meeting with the families. Seeing them all again like that. Maybe it was the killing after. That couple. It didn't feel right. Maybe because they were old. I don't fucking know. All I know is it didn't feel right.

I take out the ledger from the bottom drawer. The ones who aren't tattooed on my chest I keep track of here. I write down their names, write down the dates next to them.

Before closing it, I leaf through the pages and read some of them out loud. It's a ritual of mine. Every time I add a name, I read from the list those that felt like the couple from last night did. A remembrance of sorts. Not that they deserve it. They had a hand in my family's massacre, no matter how small.

I gave my uncle the instruction years ago. I wanted anyone who had anything at all to do with their murders, no matter what role they played. He has obliged me. He does good work. Thorough work.

But maybe the ones that don't feel right are a mistake. He's not infallible.

There's a knock on the door and I close the ledger, expecting Scarlett.

Lenore enters with another tray carrying a second coffee cup and more food. "Scarlett will be down in a few minutes. I assume she'll eat with you."

"I wasn't inviting her in for breakfast."

"Well, the girl needs to eat and if she's in your house, you're the host."

"She's not exactly a guest. Take those away."

Lenore stops, looks up at me, eyes narrowed, jaw

set. And I have a flash of memory. It's that look. The one she used when she was angry with any of us. My smile must confuse her at least momentarily before I school my features and tell her again to take Scarlett's cup and plate away.

"You listen to me, young man. Scarlett is your guest. Period. You will feed her. And you will treat her with respect."

I snort.

"If your father were here—"

"He's not here!" I snap and instantly regret it. "Fuck." I shift my gaze away then turn back to her. "I'm sorry."

"It's all right. I know how you miss them, but I'm worried about Scarlett, Cristiano."

"Why?"

"She had the window wide open when I went up there."

My heartbeat doubles at this, remembering our conversation two nights ago. "What was she doing?"

"I don't know. She said she was just taking in the sea air but I'm not sure. You just take care with her. They hurt her too, remember. They killed her parents too and God knows what else they've done to her or her brother."

It takes all I have to keep myself behind my desk.

"I don't interfere often, but this needed to be said," she adds on.

"Fine. You've said it. You can leave the things. I'll

make sure she eats. When I'm finished with her, have Alec take her down to see her brother. Jacob De La Cruz will be by in about an hour. I don't want her to see him here."

She nods without questioning me and I wonder again just how much Lenore truly knows.

I walk downstairs unattended and find Alec waiting at the bottom of the stairs.

"This way," he says.

I follow him through a corridor I've not yet explored to the last door. Alec knocks and opens it on Cristiano's command. He stands aside and I walk in to find Cristiano freshly showered, although looking like he hasn't slept, wearing a different suit than he had on yesterday. The other man is there, too, on the couch. He's sipping from a cup of coffee. Cerberus, who was lying on a bed in the corner, lopes toward me. I get the feeling I'm disturbing his morning nap.

Leaning down, I pat him.

Cristiano stands up and looks me over, then dismisses Alec. He rubs a hand over his clean-shaven face like it feels foreign to him. Maybe it is because I'd assumed the five-o'clock shadow was permanent. Actually, I hadn't realized I'd filed away so many details about his appearance and it annoys me a little that I did.

The memory of what happened last night is making my cheeks burn. Making more than that burn.

I touched myself last night. I hated myself for it, for thinking of him, for feeling his hand on me there. For remembering the feel of it. For coming at the thought of it, of him, his mouth on mine, eyes on mine, hands on me.

Blinking my gaze away, I banish the memory and concentrate on petting Cerberus who nuzzles my neck when I crouch down.

"Cerberus," Cristiano says and points to his bed.

"I don't mind."

"I do." He snaps his fingers and the dog obediently returns to his place.

"He's quite the guard dog," I say, trying to get back to our banter. Trying to pretend like what happened last night isn't on the forefront of my mind. Is it on his?

I straighten to take in the study. When I see the blanket and pillow on the edge of the couch, I wonder if he spent the night on it. It's a beautiful broken-in Chesterfield that spans the whole of one wall.

"He doesn't like most people, actually."

"I wonder where he gets that from." I smile, look to Cerberus and give him a wink. He wags his tail and I see Cristiano shake his head in my periphery. It gives me a small sense of satisfaction.

The man on the couch clears his throat and for a moment, it looks like Cristiano forgot he was even in here.

"Dante, this is Scarlett. Scarlett, my brother, Dante."

Dante nods to me but he doesn't smile, so I don't either. He doesn't like me, and I don't like him, so I guess we're good. Except that he's got a gun in a holster on his shoulder and I have nothing.

I look around the room. The study itself is beautiful, richly done like the rest of the house, with antique furnishings, a wall of books, and dark curtains to filter the sun. The scent of whiskey and Cristiano's aftershave, same as in his closet, linger in the air, making me draw out each inhale.

This little fact irritates me and when my mind wanders to last night, to our kiss, I fist my hands and squeeze my eyes shut to force the memory away.

"We'll go into Naples today to buy you some clothes."

I open my eyes, look down at myself, at the same dress I wore yesterday. I still don't know whose it is.

"How long will I be here?"

"You'll be here for the foreseeable future. Sit." I take one of the chairs in front of his desk.

I watch him put a ledger away and notice the stack of photos he's got turned upside down on one corner.

"How long will you keep Noah down in that cell?"

"I'm undecided." He pours coffee for both of us. "How do you take your coffee?"

"Black."

He pushes one of the plates of food toward me, but I don't touch it. I sip my coffee instead.

"Whose room did I sleep in?"

"Elizabeth."

"Your sister?'"

"She was only five at the time of the killings. Her best friend was sleeping over. Mara. Lenore's granddaughter. She disappeared. Just vanished into thin air. No body and we haven't been able to find any trace of her. Did your brothers ever mention a little girl?"

I shake my head, but I know what he's thinking. I'm thinking the same thing. Flesh trade. She'd be fifteen now. And the real creeps like them even younger than that.

"She's probably dead," he says but I know he doesn't believe it.

I nod half-heartedly and when I look up, his eyes are intent on mine.

"Do I need to put bars on the windows, Scarlett?"

"What?"

"Lenore said you had the window wide open."

"Your concern is touching."

"Do I?"

"I'm not going to kill myself."

"If you do, I'll throw your brother out the same window. Are we clear?"

"You'd do that, wouldn't you?"

"Who'd be in charge of the cartel now that your brothers are dead?"

Swift change of topic. "I don't know," I start. I haven't had anything to do with the actual running of things ever and I've never wanted to. "Half of them left when Diego and Angel killed our parents. The other half have probably gone to the highest bidder now that Angel and Diego are dead. They're nothing but mercenaries."

"Well, the family seems to be reuniting."

"What?"

He turns over the stack of photos and holds them out to me.

I put my coffee down and take them, flip through them. For a moment, it's like déjà vu. Our old house, a huge but cozy estate on acres of land protected by forest. I haven't seen it in ten years. I've been in Italy ever since the coup.

I touch the whitewashed wall, see the welcome mat with the once-bright red poppies on it. They were my mom's favorite flower. Her favorite color red. She told me once that dad wouldn't let her name me Poppy. He thought it was too western a name—my mom was half-American and lived most of her life in the states. She met my dad on a trip home. But he did allow Scarlett which is how I ended up with my name.

The mat is trampled now. It should be replaced. The porch, too, looks run down, the once bright yellow paint peeling off the wooden railing, weeds growing through the floorboards.

But that's not why Cristiano gave me these.

As I flip through, I see their faces. I don't recognize the younger ones but the older ones I know. Uncles and others who worked for my father. The ones who left when Diego and Angel took over.

"How did you get these?"

"Drone. You recognize them?"

"Some."

"Keep going."

I do, my heartbeat picking up because I'm sure things are about to get worse. And they do. Fast.

It's when I see the small cabin high in the mountains that my heart sinks. It's where my father held his most important meetings. Complete privacy. I don't want to know what else he did up there, but I do know if you were in real trouble with him, that's where you went. Some never came back. The ones who did were in bad shape.

But now I see it's one of my cousins, well, the husband of a cousin. One who I hadn't seen since the murders of my parents. I called him Féfé, a nickname because I couldn't say his name, Felix, when I was little. Noah couldn't either and I remember teaching him Féfé even though Felix hated it. He married my uncle Jacob's daughter.

And beside him stands Marcus Rinaldi. It's the only reason I notice Felix at all. He's an utterly unremarkable man.

I look up at Cristiano. "When were these taken?"

"Just a few days ago."

"I don't understand. Marcus is in Mexico?"

"Where is that cabin?"

"I'm not sure exactly. On De La Cruz land for sure. It's where my father held secret meetings." I leave out the rest.

"And that's Felix Pérez. Jacob's son-in-law."

I nod to confirm.

"Was he aligned with your brothers?"

"I don't know. I never saw him, but I can't be sure. But these men," I say, pointing to a few. "They walked away after the killings. They didn't trust my brothers. What's going on, Cristiano?"

"Nothing good, I'm sure." He checks his watch, stands up. "Would you like to see Noah?"

"Really?" I ask, hopeful.

He nods.

"Yes, please."

"Alec will take you down."

"Can he come up? Maybe we can just walk

outside for a little bit?"

"Not now."

"Just for as long as you say, I promise—"

"I said not now. We'll discuss it later. I have an idea."

"What idea?"

"Later. If you want to see him, now is your opportunity."

I stand, not wanting to blow it.

His eyes skim over me. "It's my mother's dress. Or so Lenore tells me. I don't remember it." He says that last part without meeting my eyes.

I look down, straighten the skirt of the dress. "Oh."

"I thought I'd remember if I saw it on you."

"I'll take her down before I go," Dante says, standing. I'd almost forgotten he was there.

"Where are you going?" Cristiano asks him.

"I need to get some things for tonight."

"You'd better show up."

"I will." Dante turns to me, the easy smile when he was talking to Cristiano disappearing. "Let's go," he says, opening the door.

I go because I want to see Noah.

Once the study door closes, Dante takes hold of my arm. He's not rough but it's unnecessary. He stops me, makes me turn to him.

"You think you've got some hold on him?"

"What?"

"You're a fuck toy to him. That's all. Don't get any fucking ideas."

I tug my arm, but he doesn't let go.

"I don't like you. And I don't trust you," he says as if I didn't already know.

"Feeling's mutual."

A flash of irritation darkens his eyes. "I've got my eye on you, Scarlett De La Cruz. And I'll do whatever I need to do to protect my brother, so watch your step."

Before I can even respond, he starts to walk us toward the hallway that will lead down to the cells. But just before we get there, I hear a familiar voice.

One that makes my skin crawl.

We both stop and turn. It's my uncle. He's here, in Cristiano's house. He turns to look at us, first at Dante, whose hand tightens on my arm like he's making a fist, then me. He's talking to a soldier.

He's obviously caught off guard when he sees me, but he recovers quickly. His eyes skim over me as do the soldier's, the latter without emotion. My heart is beating so hard against my chest all I hear is rage. Blood pumping through my veins. Pounding against my ears.

"Dante," my uncle says by way of greeting. He smiles.

I look to Dante whose expression is dark. Murderous even. Well, I guess we have one thing in common.

I take a step toward him, but Dante's hand tightens.

"Let's go," he says.

I touch the metal nail file I found in the bathroom that I strapped around my thigh. A knife would be better, but this is sharp and sturdy. It'll do the job.

But Dante tugs, hand bruising now.

The man with my uncle clears his throat. "Cristiano doesn't like to be kept waiting."

My uncle gives me a one-sided grin then disappears.

I watch him go, feel my eyes narrow.

As Dante leads me to my brother, I hear another voice from behind me. I glance back and recognize the man who had peeked his head into Cristiano's room that first morning. He doesn't see me as Dante tugs me along, but I hear my uncle stop to greet him and shake my head.

Cristiano is meeting with my uncle. My fucking uncle. If this doesn't tell me where I stand in this mess, where I stand with Cristiano, then nothing will. No matter what my stupid brain wants to make of moments like last night.

Cristiano and my uncle are aligned. That puts Cristiano firmly in the opposite corner from me. It's not that unbelievable, is it? The only unbelievable part of this is that I ever thought he'd be in mine.

15

CRISTIANO

Moments after Dante has taken Scarlett, my uncle and Jacob walk into the study. I stand, shoving my hands into my pockets.

Cerberus's low growl comes from his place in the corner. I don't comment as Jacob glances over at the hound.

"I don't know why you keep that dog," my uncle says.

"I like him," I say. "Jacob." I nod in greeting.

"Good to see you, Cristiano," Jacob says.

My uncle takes a seat and crosses his ankle over the opposite knee. He chooses the Chesterfield at the far end, away from Cerberus who lays his head back down but keeps that low growl going, eyes on my uncle.

I smile at Jacob. Well, it's an attempt at a smile. I don't like him. I don't trust him. Not even after he killed his own nephews to prove his loyalty to me. He switches sides too often. One of those mercenaries Scarlett mentioned.

"Sit," I tell him, gesturing to the chair beside the one Scarlett sat in.

He does. "I see my niece walking freely in your house."

My uncle makes a sound, but I don't turn to him. "Scarlett is not your concern."

"Watch out for that one, son."

"I'm not your son. Never call me that again."

"I'm just saying—"

"Never call me that again," I say slowly, wanting to be sure he understands.

He puts his hands up, palms to me. "All right, all right. No harm intended." He turns to David and laughs, expecting my uncle to laugh with him I guess, but he doesn't. Instead, he just looks back at Jacob, eyes flat. Unimpressed.

I wait, silent too as he returns his attention to me. He clears his throat.

"Your son-in-law met with Rinaldi," I tell him, studying his response.

Jacob sided with me against Rinaldi. He sided with me against the De La Cruz brothers. He pulled the trigger to execute them. This is an important detail. I expect him to be number one on the cartel's hitlist. He's a traitor to them.

Or he's smarter than I give him credit for.

The only thing I know for certain in this life is how cockroaches like Jacob De La Cruz manage to crawl out of their holes unscathed when the rest of the world has been razed to the ground. He's a survivor. And an opportunist.

"And I have some news from that meeting."

"Well, isn't that convenient."

"My son-in-law and I are aligned. We always have been. I am now the most powerful man in the De La Cruz Cartel and since I only have daughters, he is next in line."

"Are you now? By killing your brother and his wife along with your nephews and then executing those same nephews?"

He clears his throat.

"Italian families don't quite work that way," I say. "Explain it to me."

"I was never on board with what Rinaldi did to your family and I have never been in support of human trafficking. Rinaldi duped Diego and Angel. They were the muscle, really. Not much in the way of brains." He points to his head. "Easily manipulated. But when they offered Scarlett up to Rinaldi to seal the cartel and the mafia's union by marriage, they would have shut me out. You know this. You know what they planned for me. I was no longer useful to them. Only took a cut of the money," he pauses to study me momentarily. I just look back flatly. "I've been in touch with Felix who has kept communication open with the rest of the family. They all agreed that once Diego and Angel were out of the way, the cartel would reassemble under a new leader. Europe is a profitable route for us, after all. And with the connections and protections you and your uncle can guarantee us, well, yours is the side I am on. I'm loyal to you, Cristiano. As is Felix."

"Then what was he doing meeting with Rinaldi?"

He seems momentarily taken aback but recovers quickly. "Rinaldi was attempting to re-negotiate his contract. Remember Scarlett would have been the glue to bind us to him."

I knew this. I knew why the marriage between Scarlett and Rinaldi had to take place. But to hear it from this scum, to hear him talk about her life like it's his to be played with, it makes my blood boil.

"But he no longer has possession of her. You do," he tacks on.

Scarlett is a pawn. It's all she ever was to them. It's what she should be to me.

"Turns out you were right, Cristiano," he finishes, and I realize I'd tuned him out. He talks too much anyway.

"Right in what?"

"Keeping her alive," my uncle says, standing now, joining us and making a point of not looking at Cerberus who raises his head and tracks him across the room.

"The Cartel wants her and Noah back. Assuming the boy isn't dead yet," Jacob says.

I don't confirm one way or another. "And why do they want them back, pray tell?"

"They're blood."

"So family *is* important? I'm confused."

Jacob snorts, looks toward the bottle of whiskey. "My brother used to drink the same brand you know that?"

I glance over at it, remember how Scarlett always looks at it. "Did he?" I wonder if it reminds her of her father and I think about what Lenore said this morning. But I don't care to discuss this detail with Jacob. I want the information he has. The information he is feeding me piecemeal.

"That meeting between Rinaldi and the cartel didn't go as Rinaldi hoped. He thought he'd meet the next in charge. Pick up where Diego and Angel left off. But they know what happened. They know it was you who killed the brothers."

"Do they know you pulled the trigger?" I ask, wanting to be sure he understands his predicament and my power.

From the way his expression tightens, I know they don't.

"Not to mention the money Rinaldi owes the cartel with the cocaine shipment at the bottom of the ocean and the human cargo intercepted," he continues, not missing a beat. "All that matters is that my son-in-law is the one in charge now in Mexico and I'm in charge here."

I feel my eyebrows rise on my head. "You're in charge?"

"What I mean is that through me you have a path. The cartel knows Rinaldi is a longshot for the winning side. You hit them hard. He owes them a lot of money because it happened here. After delivery. They also know he has lost Scarlett."

"And that you have her," my uncle tacks on but I've done the math. I did it a few years ago.

"Make her your wife and you'll have the cartel's loyalty. Together, with the Cartel reinstated to nearly the numbers my brother had, you can crush Rinaldi under your foot and regain your position as the most powerful man in Italy. In all of Europe."

"And what's in it for you?" I ask Jacob.

"Me? Well, I will see my niece married. Her future secured."

"You would have executed her just two days ago, Jacob. I was there, remember?"

He smiles a smile that doesn't touch his eyes. "I'll be honest here. I don't see myself going back to Mexico. I know there are those who still blame me for going along with Diego and Angel's plans to overthrow my brother. As far as Rinaldi was concerned, I was never welcome. He had Diego and Angel. Why pay a third man? In exchange for my role in helping you secure your place with the cartel I would like to have what I need to retire comfortably. Disappear from the world so I don't have to look over my shoulder at every turn."

"You want out?" Why does that surprise me?

He nods. "I'm not young like you, Cristiano."

"Hm." I'm not sure I buy it.

"What about you, Uncle," I ask, turning to my uncle. "Have you had a change of heart about the girl?"

"It is convenient, isn't it? She's not Italian of course but, well, you'll have to settle." I feel my jaw clench, but I keep my feelings to myself. "It'll be in name alone anyway. You marry her, reinstate your original contract with the cartel. They'll agree to your rules as far as flesh trade. You'll have to make a few more examples, I'm sure, but they'll agree, isn't that right, Jacob?"

Jacob nods. "I have a list of the men who will oppose the end of the flesh trade. It's very lucrative, as you know." He takes an envelope out of his pocket and sets it on my desk.

I stand so Jacob is the only one still sitting. He slowly gets to his feet. "Shall I give my niece the good news, then?" He extends his hand for me to shake.

"Antonio will take you back to the mainland," I

tell him, pushing a button under my desk. A soldier opens the door within moments.

"Oh, all right then. Thanks."

I nod.

Jacob awkwardly tucks his hand into his pocket, says goodbye to my uncle and leaves.

"You buy that crock of shit?" I ask my uncle.

"I wouldn't trust him as far as I can throw him, no, but the facts are the facts. Marry Scarlett and you'll have sealed your deal with the cartel. It'll leave Rinaldi wide open."

"What time am I expected at the gala?" I ask, changing the subject.

"Eight. Bring the girl. Let them see her on your arm," he pauses. "How did last night go by the way?"

He means the older couple. "Like it always does."

"It's done?"

"Has it ever not been done?"

He smiles. "Let's focus on the cartel. Then we'll hit Rinaldi." He checks his watch. "I have to get back. Meeting in an hour." He walks to the door but stops. "Oh, one more thing."

"Yeah."

"I heard Lenore talking to Dante about Mara."

"Ah."

"I didn't realize he had anyone looking for her."

"She's Lenore's granddaughter. It's understandable she needs closure."

"You need to let any hope for Mara go. It's a

waste of effort and resources. She's dead, Cristiano. And better off, considering."

"Dead is never better off."

"You'll drive yourself crazy if you don't put this to rest."

I check my watch. "I'll see you tonight, Uncle."

16

SCARLETT

The first thing I see when I get upstairs is the veil. It's folded and set on the foot of the single bed I slept on last night.

Picking it up, I smell detergent and see how much whiter the lace looks. I didn't have a chance to wash it before the wedding day. The stains are gone too. No blood. Like it never even happened.

I'm glad.

Keeping it on my lap, I sit on the edge of the bed and look around. This is Elizabeth Grigori's room. Cristiano's little sister. She was five when she was killed. She'd have been fifteen now. Same age as Noah. And her little friend, what was her name? Mara. She disappeared. Seems strange if they took someone that they'd take Mara and not the daughter of their enemy.

And after all this time, I wonder if Cristiano is

still searching for her. It makes me a little sad to think of it.

But then the door opens, and I leap to my feet. No knock, but I'm not surprised.

Cristiano stands in the doorway taking up the whole of it. He looks around the room and I wonder if he's been inside here or if he avoids it. If it brings too many memories because it's still decorated for a five-year-old little girl who loved both princesses and toy cars.

He shifts his gaze to mine before it falls to the veil I'm hugging.

"Lenore cleaned it," he says, and I get the feeling again that he's not used to being around people. Having to talk to people. It's not that he's awkward. You'd have to give a fuck to be awkward. He's just abrupt.

"She did a good job. It's like new."

He nods. Cristiano is a man of very few words.

"Come out of here. I can't talk to you in here. I need to get some things anyway."

I do as he says, wondering why he put me in there at all. I walk across the hall to his bedroom, bringing the veil with me because I don't know what to do with it otherwise.

"What was my uncle doing here?"

"Nothing," Cristiano says, disappearing into the closet.

"Not nothing. Is he your partner now? Your

connection to the Cartel? Is his son-in-law running the show? Because Felix Pérez is as much a liar and an opportunist as Jacob." I give a bitter laugh. "Féfé Pérez running the show."

"Féfé?"

"I couldn't say Felix when I was little and the nickname stuck. Noah calls him that too. Also, I don't like him, and it pisses him off so..." I shrug a shoulder.

He walks out of the closet carrying a garment bag. Before I can ask what it is, he asks me if I'm ready to go.

"Shopping?"

He nods.

"Why?"

"Do you want to wear that dress day in and day out?"

"No, but—"

"Besides, we need to get you a gown."

"A gown? Why?"

"We're going to a gala tonight." He opens the bedroom door.

"A what?"

"It's a children's charity. I donated some money, and the gala should hopefully raise more."

"You donated to a children's charity?"

"Don't look so shocked. Most of it lined the pocket of a politician we need on our side."

"Ah, the angle."

"Everyone has an angle. Even you, Little Kitten. Let's go."

I walk out. "I don't have an angle."

"No?" He falls into step beside me on the stairs.

"No."

"What about getting your brother out of his cell? Isn't that your angle?"

"That's not an angle. An angle is some ulterior motive."

"And you're being nice to me because?"

I'm about to open my mouth to argue when one of his men meets us at the front door. "Chopper or boat, sir?" he asks.

"Boat. You'll follow ours. Bring Alec."

"Sir, we have—"

"Bring Alec."

"Yes, sir."

Cristiano takes his coat off the hook and realizes then I don't have one. He puts his over my shoulders.

"I'm fine," I say, trying to shrug it off. It smells like him. And it feels nice around my shoulders. Safe.

"It'll be cold on the water." He pushes it back on and we walk outside.

"Don't you need one?"

"We'll pick one up for you when we get to the shop then I can have mine back. And before you do anything stupid with it, it's one of my favorite coats."

"Got it. So, like I shouldn't throw it overboard?" I

ask as we walk out to where two speedboats are docked.

"You do and I'll throw you in to get it."

"Ha-ha."

"Water's cold this time of year."

I roll my eyes.

He holds out his hand to help me on board.

In the distance I see a sailboat, too. It's bigger than these. I look back at the house, at the island. "So, mafia business is going well? What makes the most profit? Trafficking drugs or people?"

"Get your ass on the boat, Scarlett."

I take his hand only because I have to as the water's a little choppy. "Are you sure it's safe?"

"Can you swim?"

"Are you serious? If this thing—"

"Relax. I'm fucking with you." He steps on board after pulling the ropes free that have been holding the boat to the dock. "And just so you know, I don't deal in flesh trade. My family never did."

"Oh." I study him. "Really? What is that, like a code or something? Only drugs which by the way also hurt people."

"You don't know what you're talking about and I advise you to shut the fuck up."

"I'm curious. Explain it to me."

He walks toward me, and I back up a step. "Ever hear the expression better to keep your mouth shut and let them think you're an idiot, than open it and confirm their suspicions?"

"Fuck off." I turn to walk away. He catches me by my arm and twists so I turn back to him. "Get off."

"Be careful, Little Kitten."

"Stop calling me that."

"Then put those baby claws away."

"Fuck you."

"Careful or I'm going to give you something you desperately need."

"I don't need a fuck, especially from you, thank you."

"You'll wish that's what I had in mind."

"What the hell does that even mean?"

He leans in close. "Push me again. Just one more time and I'll show you."

I glare and my mouth, oddly and completely out of character, does as my mind instructs and shuts up.

He gives me one of his signature grunts, releases me, and digs keys out of his pocket.

"So, they'll follow us?" I ask pointing to the three men who look like secret service in the next boat.

Cristiano nods and starts the engine. "You'll want to sit down."

"I'm fine," I start, and I know he jerks the boat on purpose because he grins like a wildcat when I instantly land on my butt on the floor.

"Jerk," I mutter as I maneuver to sit on one of the cushioned seats.

He gives me a smirk. "You should listen to your elders."

"What are you? Twenty-eight? Twenty-nine?"

"Twenty-seven."

"You're not an elder."

"I'm older than you. That makes me your elder."

I shake my head, reminding myself to stay focused. I want some answers about my uncle, and I want to know his idea about Noah.

"Why don't they just come with us?" I point to the boat that's following close by.

"I don't want to be crowded."

"It's not environmentally friendly of you."

He looks at me his eyebrows raised like he's asking *really*?

"What was your idea about Noah?" I ask over the sound of the engine and the slapping of the boat against the waves. "And can you slow down a little? We're going to flip."

"We won't flip. Relax."

I grip the side of the boat, knuckles white. "I don't like this."

He looks over at me, sighs and slows.

"Thank you."

"You owe me one," he says and returns his attention to steering the boat.

I watch him. Look at his broad, powerful shoulders as I slip my arms into his jacket. It's cool on the water, almost cold, but he looks relaxed. My gaze slips lower to his ass and I remember seeing him naked. How I felt him hard against me last night.

I remember how he tasted like caramel and whiskey when he kissed me, and I remember how he looked with his eyes closed. Like our kiss was sustenance. Air.

"Noah will work for me," Cristiano says, interrupting that train of thought.

"What?"

"Noah. He'll train to become a soldier." He looks back at me.

"He's fifteen. He hasn't even finished high school."

"He'll live in my house. Be educated. Have time to prove himself trustworthy. I won't kill a kid, Scarlett. And from what I can tell of the boy, he could use a father figure."

I snort. "Like you're a good influence?"

"Better than your brothers or uncle."

"That's not a very high bar. He's too young. I don't want that."

"I'm not asking your permission. I've already spoken with him and he's very enthusiastic."

"What? When?"

"Early this morning."

"You mean he knew when I came to visit him?" He didn't say a word.

"I made him swear not to say anything."

"Let me guess, a test of loyalty." He slows the

boat as we near the port and I stand, walking over to him. I guess he told me his plan out on the water so I wouldn't attack him. I don't quite have my feet under me.

Cristiano nods, pockets the key and climbs out, then extends his hand to me.

"I'm fine. I'll get out on my own."

"Don't be stubborn."

"I'm fine."

"It's the only way, Scarlett."

I shove his hand away. "No, it's not. You can let him go. That's another way. He won't come after you and you know it." I look at my options, reaching for a pole for balance. But the wake of our security detail's boat catches me off guard, making our boat bob wildly, and sending me toppling.

I scream, anticipating the splash of cold water or worse, the crashing of my face against the pole. Just as I feel the scrape on my forehead, strong hands grab the back of the coat I'm wearing, lifting me, setting me on the dock. The coat slips off my arms. I stumble when he releases me, so he catches me again, this time keeping hold of me.

"Jesus Christ. Are you hell bent on falling in?"

I'm panicked and can't answer right away.

He must see it on my face because he exhales, shakes his head and pulls me close.

For a moment, I think he's going to hug me. To

comfort me. And I'm not sure what I'd do if he did that.

But he stops just short.

He pushes my hair back from my face, brushes his fingers over my forehead. "Just a scratch." He holds me at arm's length, squeezing my biceps. "You're too fucking stubborn for your own good. You could have knocked your head into that pole."

I touch the spot that feels a little tender, but my fingers come away clean.

"I don't like boats."

"I wouldn't put you on it if it wasn't safe."

"It clearly wasn't safe."

"It was fine. You decided to be an idiot."

"I'm not an idiot. You just told me you're recruiting my fifteen-year-old brother to become a soldier. What kind of life will he have? I wanted to get him out of it, not embed him more deeply into it. It's not fair, Cristiano. Not for him. Just let him go. Even if you keep me. Let him go."

He doesn't answer right away and for one millisecond I wonder if he's considering it. But he gives a shake of his head. "I can't do that, and you know it."

"Sir," a voice interrupts and I look up to find three SUVs lined up with men beside each one.

"Be right there, Antonio," Cristiano says, handing him the discarded coat.

Antonio walks away and Cristiano turns to me.

He wipes away the tears that I'm not sure are falling because of my near surprise swim or my getting upset about Noah.

"You're all right. You're safe."

I shove his hands away. "I'm not upset because I don't feel safe. I haven't been safe in ten years. I'm upset because nothing will change. I'm upset because maybe it would have been better if you'd just had my uncle pull that trigger two more times." I don't mean it. Why did I say it?

"Dead is never better, Scarlett. Never."

"I mean, ultimately, that's what's going to happen to my brother. To me."

"God you're fucking dramatic." He pulls me toward the second SUV.

"Fuck you." I resist all the way, and no one does a thing. Not one of the men gathered here. Not that I expect them to.

He sighs, wraps his hands around my waist and lifts me into the backseat. He rests his hands on my thighs and even for as high as the vehicle is, I still have to look up at him.

"Isn't it better than locking him up in that cell?" he asks.

I try to shove his hands away, but just then he cocks his head, glances down.

Shit.

He must feel the file I strapped to my leg. It

seems so stupid now as he pushes the dress up a little on my thigh.

"What have we here, Little Kitten?" He takes the file out of its makeshift strap constructed out of hair ties and tests the point. He looks at me, eyebrows raised, then turns to the man behind him. "We'll need a minute, Antonio."

"Yes, sir," Antonio says, turning his back as Cristiano climbs into the backseat and closes the door.

I fold my arms across my chest.

"What did you think you'd accomplish with this?"

"I don't know, poke an eye out maybe?"

He smiles.

No, it's more of a smirk.

He sets the file aside but before I can even register what's happening, he flips me face down over his lap and smacks my ass so hard I cry out in shock.

"You need to learn to behave," he says, adjusting my position, tucking me closer to him and smacking my other cheek.

"Ow! Let me up!"

"Not happening, Little Kitten," he says just before flipping my skirt up.

He stops short the instant he does, sucking in a breath. Because I'm not wearing underwear. I didn't have any.

"Let me up!" I reach back to at least cover my butt and he grabs both wrists in one hand.

"What's this?" I hear laughter in his voice.

"I didn't have underwear, you jerk! Let me up!"

He tsks and when I kick my legs, he shifts his to trap them between his thighs.

"We'll put panties on our shopping list," he says calmly before spanking me three times. "Although I'm tempted not to."

I crane my neck to look up at him. He's trying hard to keep a serious expression on his face. "Stop it. I mean it. And this is in no way funny." My face feels hot.

"It's funny from my vantage point." He raises his hand to smack again and I squeeze everything tight, my eyes, my fists, my butt.

"What do you want from me?" I call out as I process the sting.

"Well, I'd like to turn your pretty little ass bright red for starters."

"You're a fucking Neanderthal." I try to kick, but it does no good.

"And you have a very nice ass, Scarlett."

"Fuck off."

"Look at me."

"No."

"No?" He smacks again and tears sting my eyes. Then he starts rubbing my butt in lazy circles and my wires must cross because all I should feel is pain.

Pain and humiliation and brutal injustice. But his hand on me right now, him holding me like he is, that's not all I feel.

"Look at me," he repeats.

I do, a tear sliding down the side of my face.

"What did you think you'd do with a nail file strapped to your thigh like you're some warrior woman?"

"What do you expect me to do? Not fight? Not try to defend myself? I was twelve when I started fighting. I don't know any other way to be. Don't expect me to roll over for you in a day. It's not how I'm wired. I know I'm not a warrior woman. I know you're stronger than me and that you'll probably beat me every time, but I have to try."

"I don't want to hurt you, Scarlett."

"Yeah right, that's obvious. I fucking hate you."

He shakes his head and raises his arm.

I struggle, wriggle to get free, and that's when I feel him. Feel his hardness against me. He's aroused.

He's fucking aroused.

And I have no idea what the fuck is happening here in the backseat of this SUV but it's not what should be happening. It's not me hating him.

I don't speak. I don't even breathe. Looking straight ahead at the door handle, I just feel his length and don't move. I clench my butt cheeks and my fists and try not to panic because it could be worse than a spanking. He could do so much worse and no one would help me.

"Scarlett?"

I think he's been saying something but all I hear is my name. I don't answer. I can't.

"Hey," he says, leaning his face down a little.

I shake my head, trying to muffle a sniffle.

"Christ," he mutters and in the next moment, he frees my legs, and hauls me upright. He lifts me onto his lap, keeping my wrists trapped behind me.

I lean my face down to wipe away tears on his shirt. Stupid fucking tears.

Fuck.

He just spanked me. He just saw my bare ass, spanked it and he got hard doing it. He's still hard and I can't even begin to process what I'm feeling.

I wipe my nose on his shoulder too because he deserves it. "Let me go," I say, not looking at him. It's not fully out of embarrassment either. I don't want him to see the confusion in my eyes because he seems to read me like a book.

He cups my face, which I'm sure is as red as my butt, forcing my gaze to his, then wipes a tear with his thumb. "I don't want to hurt you, Scarlett."

"You liked doing it. You got hard doing it." I twist, but it's no use.

"I'm a man."

I snort.

"Listen to me and I'll let you go," he says quietly, no laughter in his tone.

"Why should I?"

"Because you need to know that I mean it. That I don't want to hurt you."

"My butt will disagree."

He smiles and it's not a nasty smirk or like he's laughing at me. It's almost a boyish one. "If I really wanted to hurt you, you'd be down in one of those cells right now or worse. And as stubborn as you are, you're smart enough to know that's true."

I swallow, twisting my arms but still he doesn't budge.

"You have enemies, Scarlett. You and Noah both."

"I know. I'm sitting with one."

"I mean enemies who will do real damage. You know this. Tell me you know this."

I can't deny it, but I don't want to confirm it either, so I grit my teeth and stay silent.

"I'm not going to hurt you or Noah as long as you don't give me cause to."

"What does that mean?"

"It's simple." His expression goes dead serious. "It means don't betray me."

"You'd have to have someone's trust to betray them. You and I do not have each other's trust."

"Not yet. But I'm a pretty good judge of character and I hope you'll be trustworthy."

I snort.

"Will you? Because I can name at least two men who'd love to get their hands on you. If they did, it wouldn't be pretty."

"So what? You're helping me? Is that what you want me to believe? Maybe I should be grateful to you?"

"This is serious."

"You think I don't know that? You think watching my brothers executed didn't clue me in?"

He squeezes my wrists. "You are so god damned stubborn." He shakes his head, looks away momentarily. "I'm helping me and if in the process that helps you then so be it. I have vowed to avenge my family's murders. My mother's assault. And even given your name, I don't believe you or your brother should be punished."

"Well, thanks. It's big of you to acknowledge since I was twelve and he was five at the time."

"Christ—"

"If we shouldn't be punished then why not let us go?"

"I can't. And you don't want me to. You know what's waiting for you out there. You're safest under my protection."

"I'm not safe and neither is my brother."

"Not on your own. You're right about that." He's dead serious and the way he looks at me, it's unnerving. I almost can't keep eye contact because he's really looking at me. Seeing something inside me. "Are you all right, Scarlett?"

"Apart from enduring this latest humiliation, I'll be fine."

He lets go of my wrists and slides me to the bench before strapping me in.

"I'm not in agreement about Noah. I'm just not," I say.

"Then you need to find a way to accept it. There is no alternative."

I turn my gaze out the window because I'm crying again. Stupid. I don't even know why. I should just be angry. I should just want to claw his eyes out.

"Do you need a minute?"

I shrug a shoulder, refusing to look at him. I'm unable to speak because my throat has closed up and I know if I open my mouth, I'll just sob, and I can't do that. Not now. Not in front of him. And I'm relieved when, without another word, he knocks on the window signaling the driver who gets in behind the wheel. We head off to wherever it is we're going.

17

CRISTIANO

H er reaction wasn't what I expected. I took her over my lap because it wouldn't do serious damage, but it would chasten her. But to think I wouldn't get hard doing it was my bad. And I knew the instant she felt me.

It's been a few hours and she's been moping along all afternoon, trying on whatever I pick out and refusing to look at me. I assumed she'd enjoy spending the day shopping. Don't all women love to shop?

Maybe she's embarrassed at what happened in the SUV but she needs to get over it. Even if her feelings are half as confused as mine.

I'm not apologizing for what I did. It needed to be done.

She needs to behave tonight. She needs to behave every night. And I meant what I said. I do hope she'll be trustworthy because I don't want to hurt her.

I was twelve when I started fighting. I don't know any other way to be.

Her words repeat while I study her as she eats the last of her pasta. She still has an appetite. A good sign even if she hasn't said one word to me in the last four hours. She's processing and it's a lot to take in. I have no doubt when I tell her about our upcoming nuptials, she'll fight me again. In a way, I feel sorry for her but neither she nor I have a choice in the matter.

"Would you like dessert?" I ask once she's finished and the waiter clears our plates.

"No."

"No, *thank you*."

She narrows her eyes, leans back in her chair and stubbornly sits there staring at me.

I lean toward her. "What is it, Little Kitten?"

She narrows her eyes at me. "How much longer is this shopping trip going to take?"

"You have somewhere to be?"

"Pretty much anywhere you're not."

"That's too bad." My phone rings then. It's Charlie. "Excuse me." I stand and walk away from the table to take the call. "Charlie?"

"There's some noise about tonight."

"What noise?"

"Not sure exactly yet but I talked to Antonio about doubling security."

"Rinaldi?"

"I don't know."

"All right." I take a breath in, glance at Scarlett.

"I'll let you know as soon as I learn more," he says.

"Thanks, Charlie. I'll drop by later, too. I have a couple more names for you."

He's silent for a long moment. "I'll be here."

We disconnect and I dial my uncle. He answers on the third ring.

"I'm going to send Scarlett your way earlier than expected," I say. "I'll come later."

"Something up?"

"Not sure."

"All right. I'll be expecting her."

We disconnect and I go back to the table, checking my watch and signaling for Alec to come over.

"Sir?" Alec asks.

"Change of plans," I tell him then turn to Scarlett. "You have one more stop to make before Alec takes you to my uncle's house in the city."

She looks up at Alec then at me. "You're not coming with me?"

"I thought you didn't want to be with me."

"I guess I'd choose you over your uncle. I don't

know him, but I already know not to count that as a big win for you."

"Slow learner, aren't you?"

"Will your brother be there too? Because that would be a real treat."

I sigh. "Dante is protecting his family. He has nothing against you personally."

"Yeah, right. Can I just go back to the island?"

"I already told you we have an event tonight. Alec, you'll take her to the boutique. Mrs. Sorani has chosen some dresses. She'll have the final say on the dress then you're to take her to the house. I'll meet you there later. I have people scheduled to come to the house at a little after five to get her ready. Make sure she complies with anything they might need." That last part I say to her.

"Yes, sir," she says with a salute, mimicking my soldiers. I let it slide.

"You're not to leave her side, understood?" I tell Alec.

He nods.

I take out my wallet and drop some bills on the table, more than enough to cover our lunch and the revenue the owner lost to close while hosting only us. I push my chair back and stand. Scarlett looks uncertainly from me to Alec and back. I'm surprised at her bravado. She is out of her league and out of her element and she knows it.

"I'll walk her out," I tell Alec who takes the hint and leaves.

Walking around to Scarlett's side, I stand behind her seat. Leaning over to place my hands over her forearms, resting on the arms of the chair. I inhale, take in the soft perfume of a feminine shampoo. Lenore's doing, I'm sure.

She turns her head a little, leaning away just enough so we're not cheek to cheek. I see how her pulse drums against her neck and hear her swallow.

"Are you going to be good? Or are you going to give me the opportunity to take you over my knee again for a real spanking?"

She flushes, blinks rapidly before returning her gaze to mine. "If you touch me like that again I'll kill you in your sleep."

"But you wouldn't mind me touching you another way?"

"I mean it. I'll kill you."

I smile wide. "I have no doubt you'd try. Truce, all right?"

"Truce? You don't need to make a deal with me. I'm your prisoner. You have enough soldiers that if I take one step in the wrong direction, I'm sure I'll be surrounded in an instant, weapons trained on me."

"My men know not to train their weapons on you."

She seems surprised, at least momentarily. "And you have my brother. You don't need to make a truce with me, Cristiano. I'll do what you say, and you know it, so don't pretend to want to do right by me."

"I'm not pretending."

"Noah needs clothes too if he's going to stay on the island."

"Already sorted." I release her and pull her chair out. "You'll see them at the next shop. If anything is missing add it to the order."

She bites the inside of her cheek. I guess she's trying to come up with some quip, but she doesn't say anything.

"Ready?" I ask her.

She opens her mouth, closes it again and stands. I walk her out to Alec and the others, opening the door and lifting her into the SUV.

"I can get into a car myself."

I put my hands on her thighs like earlier. "You didn't sneak a knife out, did you? An ice pick, maybe?"

She bites the inside of her cheek to keep from smiling and it makes me smile.

"I'll see you tonight, Scarlett."

Alec gets into the front seat and I give Scarlett one last look before stepping back to close the door.

18

SCARLETT

I'm surprised about the things for Noah but true to his word, bags of clothes were waiting for my approval at the next shop. Although if he truly is keeping him on the island, I'm sure he doesn't want him wearing the same clothes that are stained with Diego and Angel's blood, so this isn't exactly selfless of Cristiano.

It's late afternoon by the time we get to Cristiano's uncle's house, on the edge of the city. And house isn't quite the word. It's a mansion, a proper Italian mansion set well back from the beautiful stone pillars cradling ornate iron gates that open to let us in. The grounds are elegantly manicured and before a servant opens the front door, I can hear the sounds of someone playing piano inside.

Alec enters behind me. I take a moment to look around, take in the elegant, monied feel of the place.

Our home in Mexico was always more cozy than elegant. We lived in that house, played in every room. The sounds of children and the smells of cooking constant. This place, for as beautiful as it is, is cold. Lifeless. And when Cristiano's uncle turns a corner, I wish Cristiano were here at my side. I wish he'd stand bastion between me and this man, because from where I stand, I already feel his animosity toward me.

"Welcome, Scarlett De La Cruz," he says, drawing out my name while looking me over and not trying too hard to hide the fact that I'm not actually welcome.

I glance at Alec at my side. He's carrying some bags but most of the things are loaded in the SUVs.

"I'm David Grigori, Cristiano's uncle."

"I know who you are."

"Come in." He turns to Alec, looks at the bags. "Joanna," he calls out.

A woman appears out of nowhere.

"Take those things to Ms. De La Cruz's room."

She nods and relieves Alec of the bags, then disappears up the stairs.

"You can wait with the others," David tells Alec.

"I'm to stay with her at all times. Cristiano's orders."

"Well, Cristiano isn't here, is he? And you're in my house. Soldiers don't belong in my house."

"Sir, I—"

The man who opened the door for us, opens it again.

"I'll let you know if we require your assistance," David tells Alec who looks at me hesitatingly then nods to David and leaves.

So much for that.

I clear my throat when David turns his gaze back to me. "Big day?" he asks.

I shrug a shoulder and don't bother to smile. "When is Cristiano getting here?"

"He'll see you at the ball."

"He said he'd be here."

"I guess something more important came up." He walks a circle around me, and I don't know what to do but stand there. "Has he fucked you yet?"

I turn my gaze to him. "Excuse me?"

He comes to stand in front of me. "My nephew. Has he fucked you yet?"

Is he for real?

"The look on your face tells me he hasn't. Which explains why you're not using the servant's entrance."

"I'm happy to use any entrance that doesn't include having to talk to you."

He snorts, looks almost amused. "I suppose he has to tolerate you, though, considering. Even if you are Cartel trash."

I have no words and it's rare that I'm left speechless.

"I don't like you, Scarlett. I don't like your family. If it were up to me, you, your brother and your uncle would be six feet under with the rest of them. You destroyed that boy."

I know I shouldn't care what he says or what he thinks, but that last sentence hits me, and I know he's right, at least about that.

"But it turns out you may prove useful after all."

"What does that mean?"

"Don't you know?"

"Know what?"

He grins. "I'll let my nephew take care of that. Take off your jacket."

"What?"

He holds out his hand. "Jacket. I don't suppose you need to wear it indoors."

I should tell him to fuck off but instead I take off my jacket. By the time I hand it to him, his expression has changed, gone from cold and calculated to angry.

And it's not me he's looking at. It's the dress I'm wearing.

"Where did you get that dress?" he asks, his tone low, rage barely controlled.

I look down at it, wonder what's wrong with it. "Lenore gave it to me."

"It's not yours. Take it off."

"What?"

"You heard me. Take it off," he says through

gritted teeth.

"Fine. Just let me go to my room. I have something to change into—"

"Now!"

I almost jump at that. "No. No way." I glance back at the door where the servant, who probably doubles as security from the look of him, stands.

"Don't make me tear it off you."

"I just—"

He grabs hold of my arm, his grip painful. "Take. It. Off."

"Why?"

He drags his gaze from the dress. "Because it belonged to Melinda. He shouldn't have given you one of her dresses."

Melinda. Cristiano's mom.

Just then Joanna returns into the living room. "The women from the salon are ready, sir."

He doesn't take his eyes off me. "The dress. Now."

I reach back to undo the zipper, just wanting to get out of here now, knowing he's not going to let me walk out of this room without giving it to him this second. He releases me when I pull it off. At least he doesn't look at me with leering eyes as I hold it out to him. Using my other arm to cover my breasts, I'm grateful Cristiano bought me both bra and panties on our shopping spree.

If Joanna thinks it's at all strange, she doesn't let

on. David takes the dress and looks at me once more. I'm grateful it's only contempt I see in his eyes.

"Don't leave your room until I come for you, am I clear?" he asks, tone scratchy, hateful.

"Crystal."

"Joanna," he barks.

"This way, Miss."

Keeping one arm strapped over my breasts, I follow her up the stairs and to my room where women are setting up what looks to be a mobile salon. Joanna holds out a robe for me as soon as we're inside.

"Here you go," she says.

I take it. It takes me a minute to thank her because I'm not expecting this kindness. How long has it's been since I've expected anything resembling kindness?

She nods, not quite meeting my eyes but the look on her face tells me she's embarrassed at having witnessed that.

I pull the robe on, sitting where the women tell me to sit and just tuning everything out. I try to make myself go numb, which is getting harder and harder to do because all I can think is that Cristiano is the closest thing to an ally that I have right now. I need him, need his protection. Because I know he's all that's standing between me and a grave.

But it's more than that.

And it would be less complicated if it weren't.

19

CRISTIANO

"He'll be pissed but I don't care. I want men riding with my uncle and Scarlett. How many are on property?"

"Thirteen, sir. I'm seeing if I can get some on the roof without raising eyebrows," Antonio says. "Don't worry, we've got it covered. If it becomes more than a threat, we'll take care of it."

"And get her out. Understand?"

"Yes, sir."

I disconnect the call and dial my uncle. I'm on my way to the event location but am later than I hoped. I had two things to do when I left Scarlett after lunch. First, pick up the rings. Wedding bands. Simple. That's what I should have stuck to, at least.

But for some fucking reason and by some stupidity, I'd brought my mother's engagement ring with me and had it resized for her.

I touch my pocket now, feel the velvet box and I'm not sure what the fuck is wrong with me when it comes to this woman. Why the fuck am I giving her this particular engagement ring when what she'll want to do is use the stones to carve out my eyes as soon as she hears what will be expected of her.

"Cristiano," my uncle says, picking up on the fourth ring. "We didn't need the goddamned detail. I have my own security."

"I'm not taking any chances. She's with you?"

A pause. "Yes."

"Can she hear us?"

"Of course not. What's going on?"

"Something's going down tonight."

"I haven't heard anything from my sources."

"Where's Alec?"

"Riding with my men."

"I told him not to leave her side."

"It gets a little cramped in the limo."

"Fine. Don't mention anything to her. I don't want her worried."

"I wouldn't. Where did you go anyway?"

"Picking up a ring," I leave the rest out.

"All afternoon? Aren't you the romantic?"

"I'll see you in a few minutes." I disconnect the call and tuck it into my pocket, thinking about my second task this afternoon which was dropping by Charlie's to give him those names.

I've been giving him the names I write in my

ledger. The ones that just didn't feel right to me. I told him the first time I brought them to him to dig up as much dirt as he could. Maybe it's a way of alleviating my conscience. If I know they're bad people, it will make what I did a little more okay. Without concrete evidence of their involvement in my family's murders, things just don't sit right sometimes.

And I know my uncle won't always have concrete evidence.

I won't tell him about giving Charlie the names for a couple of reasons. First, Charlie and my uncle do not like each other. They're civil when they need to be, but something happened between them years ago, must be fifteen years now, and neither of them has moved on from it.

Second, I know my uncle would find it weak that I need to do this. That I need to clear my conscience.

The driver pulls through the gates of the mansion where the party is being hosted. It's a private home and I can't march in with a detail of security guards without raising the alarm that I'm back in business. The Grigori Mafia restored; all nefarious activities resumed. That wouldn't look good for the charity.

The moment I step out of the vehicle the two women from the charity appear to accompany me inside. I smile and go along, not hiding the fact that I'm checking my watch.

The first person I see when I step inside is Jacob De La Cruz. It turns my already dark mood black.

"Excuse me," I tell the ladies and unlink my arms.

Jacob smiles, turning to say something to the bartender, so just when I reach him, a whiskey is set on the counter for me.

"I had your preferred brand stocked," he says.

"What are you doing here?" I take the whiskey, thank the bartender. Not this asshole.

"Since I'm leaving the business, I thought it would be good to rub elbows with this...um...better class of people."

I swallow some of the whiskey. "There is no better class of people, Jacob. I thought you'd know that by now."

"Where's my niece?"

The way he calls her *my* niece bugs me. Why not just call her Scarlett?

"On her way."

"Did you tell her the good news yet?"

I open my mouth to answer when his gaze shifts to the door. I swear the air around me shifts and sparks like it's electric. Alive and humming.

She's here. I feel it.

But something in Jacob's expression has caught my attention. His jaw is tight, body stiffening. There's something not right about the way he's looking at her. At *his fucking niece.*

I blink, turn my head and the instant I see her from across the huge room, my breath catches.

Every man in the place has stopped to look at her and I want to punch every single one of them. I can't blame them, however, can I? She's fucking beautiful.

Scarlett is standing just inside the entrance, my uncle at her side. She's looking around the room, lips slightly parted wearing a gown the color of her name. Silk hugs her curves, breasts lifted, nipples poking against the fabric, the slit that splits the dress exposing a toned, slender thigh. It's just this side of modest.

I'd send the boutique owner a bonus if I hadn't already seen the charge on my card.

She finally spots me, the dark, smoky liner making her eyes a soft gold. Like sand. The color of the beach on the island when the summer sun hits it.

Her lips are painted to match the dress and her hair is piled on top of her head. I know every man in here has a hard-on for her and every woman wants to be her.

That or kill her.

They'd have to get in line. My Little Kitten has more enemies than she knows.

My phone buzzes in my breast pocket. My uncle puts his hand on her elbow and she abruptly tugs it away. I'm glad. I don't want him touching her.

"Beautiful, isn't she?" Jacob asks beside me.

I turn to find him studying me with a smirk on his face, looking more relaxed than I've probably ever seen him.

"Shame what her brothers did to her."

He's baiting me. I know it. But I bite. "What do you mean?"

"Oh," he says, trying too hard for casual as he gives a shake of his head. "Nothing."

"What do you mean, Jacob. You clearly want to tell me something."

He smiles. It's not a kind smile. "Making a whore out of her like they did." When his eyes fall on Scarlett again, there's a leering look inside them. It makes my skin crawl. I'm about to grab this asshole and shake him, smash his face into the bar. Maybe stab his perverted eyes out with an ice pick.

But I need to keep calm.

"What do you mean?" I ask again, swallowing some whiskey to occupy my mouth before I give anything away.

"Rinaldi wanted a taste. They were smart though. I have to give them that." He turns to the man behind the bar. "Bartender. Another for me and my friend."

I can't help myself. I grab hold of his collar because in my periphery I see my uncle leading her toward us and I want to know what the fuck this son-of-a-bitch is talking about.

"Spit it out, Jacob. What the fuck are you trying to tell me?"

He looks down at my hand and it takes me a minute, but I release him.

"Rinaldi wanted Scarlett from the beginning. Had a thing for her. The brothers thought if he fucked her, he wouldn't marry her. But without the marriage, their position would be weakened. Having a look, however, well, that seemed to satisfy his lust. Building anticipation until the wedding night I guess."

"What the hell are you talking about?"

He turns to look at her, expression hardening. "Let's just say that pig knows every inch of her." He returns his gaze to me. "It was good for her pride, though. As you probably know, she's prideful, my niece. The night her brothers sold her virginity in exchange for the marriage of the two families brought her down a notch. Several."

Rage beats against my ears, my chest, my finger-nails digging into my palms.

"How do you know this?" I ask through gritted teeth.

"Oh, I was there. And really, that was all assuming she was a virgin at all. I was around when she was growing up. I remember how she pranced around in her tight little shorts when she was just a girl."

What the fuck is this asshole saying?

"Always putting on a show for any man who walked by."

He turns to me, must see the rage building inside me because he clears his throat. "I tried to help her, of course."

I turn just as Scarlett is within earshot. "I'm sure you tried to help her," I say under my breath, vowing then to kill this pervert. Not even caring about the cartel and what that would do to my relationship with them. I will kill Jacob De La Cruz.

I step toward Scarlett and my uncle, blocking Jacob's view of her, not wanting him to look at her any longer. I can't stand the thought that even his eyes should fall on her.

I was twelve when I started fighting. I don't know any other way to be.

At least I was an adult.

"Cristiano." My uncle nods in greeting and walks past me to the bar. I don't care.

"You look beautiful," I tell her, part of me wanting to put my jacket over her shoulders to hide her from her uncle. From the other ogling men.

She looks up at me like she has a hundred things to say. Like she wants to curse me to hell and fall into my arms all at once.

"Why is he here? Why are you talking to him?" she asks, eyes just flashing to Jacob momentarily.

I put my hand at her lower back, turn her away, walking at an angle to shield her from him.

"He's an asshole, Scarlett. I know that. You don't have to worry about him."

"An asshole like your uncle, you mean?"

Someone interrupts us. The women from the charity again, like fucking gnats, these two. They start talking like we're not having a private fucking conversation. What the fuck is wrong with people?

"Excuse us," I say and walk Scarlett toward a quieter corridor. "What happened with my uncle?"

"He lost his shit when he saw me in your mom's dress. I'm not going there again. I don't care what you say. I'm not." Her eyes get shiny and although I hear anger in her voice, she's vulnerable.

"He loved my mother. I'm sure it was hard for him to see—"

"Don't. Just don't," she turns like she's going to walk away but I grab her arm.

"Scarlett—"

"I have to use the lady's room," she says.

"How exactly did he lose his shit?" I get the feeling I'm not going to like this part.

"Let me go."

I look down at my hand around her arm. Bruises have already formed there. Did I put them there? Fuck. I loosen my grip, then release her altogether.

She rubs her arm. "You want to hear what an asshole your uncle is? Fine. He made me strip off the dress. Right there in the hallway. In front of him and one of his soldiers and—"

"He did what?" My brain rattles in my skull and I swear the fucking room goes sideways.

My phone begins its vibration again. Jesus fucking Christ.

I take my eyes off her for a second to quiet it and she slips away, swift to weave through the crowd and disappear around the corner.

I get as far as two steps after her only to be met by my uncle. "Lose her already?" he asks, half-joking.

"What did you do to her?"

"What did she say I did?" he asks, eyebrows to high heaven.

"The dress."

"Ah." He nods, drinks a big swallow of his whiskey. "I admit that was not my best moment."

This throws me. I don't know what I expected. "You admit it?'"

"I made her strip it off. I shouldn't have done that but seeing her in it, it did something to me. Why would you give her one of your mother's dresses, Cristiano? For fuck's sake, why hers?"

Because I wanted to see if I could remember. But I don't tell him that. "You'll apologize to her."

"Excuse me?"

"You heard me."

"Look here—"

"She's a human being."

"She's cartel trash. The same blood as those who

executed your family." His expression turns ugly. "Who assaulted your mother."

I wipe spittle off my face and take a deep breath in. "How did you know that?"

"Are you fucking serious right now?"

"That detail about mom. How did you know?" It's like fire is coursing through my veins. I want to smash something. Someone.

Lying on that floor watching it, watching what that bastard did to her, impotent to help the one time she needed me to help her. Fuck, it fucking kills me, that detail. That one fucking detail.

I rub the back of my neck, agitated. I can't think about that. Not now. Not here.

My phone goes off again, but I ignore it.

"I had it taken out of the official report, you know that. I told you that. I didn't want her humiliated in death like she was in life," my uncle says. "Now as far as Scarlett, remember what she is. A means to an end. Family first. We're not like them, not like the cartels who can execute their own. Don't let her turn your head. Make you forget even that. She'll exploit your weaknesses if you let her. You need to fuck her and get her out of your system so you can get your focus back. Get your head out of your ass, Cristiano."

"I haven't lost my focus."

"No?"

"Where's Dante?" I ask, realizing my brother isn't here.

"Something came up in the Milan office. I thought you wouldn't mind if I asked him to take care of it." My uncle has offices all over Italy and I know my brother's been working with him in the years I was incapacitated. He's grooming Dante to take over his businesses although I'm not sure what Dante wants.

"No, I don't mind," I say because he is safer away from me, away from any ties to the mafia family he came from.

We're interrupted then by someone who knows my uncle. I'm amazed at how quickly my uncle dons the mask of ease, a smile that looks so fucking real that it makes me wonder if I imagined what just happened. How he looked. What he said.

When my phone vibrates in my pocket for the hundredth time, I excuse myself and head in the direction of Scarlett as I answer.

"What is it?" I ask Antonio.

"I've been trying to get hold of you. We've got a problem."

20

SCARLETT

I'm heading toward the lady's room when I see Jacob leering at me from the opposite corner of the room. He raises his glass to me, the sea of people between us his only protection as far as I'm concerned because Cristiano hasn't come after me.

I change direction and head toward him, wishing I had that nail file to stab him in the eye. I know it wouldn't kill him but I'm good with maiming him for life. For now, at least.

As I approach, he stops a passing waiter and takes two champagne flutes off his tray. He holds one out to me.

"There she is," he says, a smile on his face. This man who just days ago was ready to pull the trigger and kill Noah and me. The man who executed Diego and Angel.

I want to slap that champagne out of his hands

but when I'm close enough, he must see my intent, because he sets both glasses down and squares his shoulders to meet me.

"You look stunning," he says, his eyes moving slowly over me, pausing at my breasts. "Your tits are practically on display, though."

"You're disgusting."

He shrugs a shoulder. "You have a bad habit of attracting men who'll do that to a woman. Make a whore of her. What does that say about you, I wonder?"

I step into his space. I'm only a few inches shorter than him and I make a point of looking him right in the eye. This bastard doesn't scare me. Not anymore. I wonder when that happened. Maybe the day I became less afraid of dying than I did of living.

"I'm going to kill you one day, Uncle."

He laughs outright. "I don't think so."

"When you least expect it, I'm going to drive a knife into your stomach and I'm going to twist slowly, so slowly, slicing all the way up to your heart so it lasts a long, long time. I'm going to watch your life slip away. I'm going to soak my hands in your blood."

He laughs. It's a nervous laugh, though. He was always a coward hiding behind my father. He's not actually a blood relative. He married my aunt, my father's sister, and took her last name in deference to my father.

"You're not being very nice, Scarlett, when I was just sticking around to congratulate you. Boring, these fundraisers."

"Congratulate me on what?"

"Your upcoming nuptials, of course. And here I thought Cristiano was just your rebound guy."

"What the hell are you talking about?"

He cocks his head to the side like he's shocked. "Did I ruin the surprise? Hasn't he asked yet? Well, proposed." His face hardens. "You'll do as you're told. For the cartel. But then again, you did always like something hard between your legs. At least if you're married, they won't call you a whore anymore. I should warn you though," he leans in close, "he's probably expecting a virgin."

I draw my arm back to slap him but before I can, a loud explosion goes off somewhere nearby. The ground beneath me shakes. The lights blink once, twice and the room goes dark.

Men and women scream, running haphazard around us.

My uncle grasps my arms hard. I stumble back, instinctively wanting to be away from him, but there's a strange look on his face. I feel something warm on the skin of my chest, my face, as his hands fall away and he drops first to his knees, then completely prone on the ground.

I stare at him, watch blood pool around him. I look down at my arms. At the red that stains them.

Blood.

Blood again.

I wipe my face with the back of my hand.

A woman bumps into me and gunshots ring out, panic everywhere, and all I can do is look at my uncle on the floor. Then someone body slams me, knocking the air out of me and taking me to the ground.

"Stay down!" It's Cristiano, his full weight on me making it hard to breathe. Machine gun fire ricochets all around us.

I crane my neck to look at him and see he's got a pistol in his hand. It's deadly but it's not a machine gun. More bullets shatter what glass remains as Cristiano points to a door.

"We're moving," he says over the noise, and simultaneously gets to his feet. He bends to keep low creating a cocoon around me as we rush toward that door.

Bullets whip by. Cristiano lets out a grunt, his step faltering only momentarily but an instant later, cold air assaults me. I realize one shoe is gone when I step onto gravelly pavement. Alec takes hold of me and two men flank him, all with heavy weapons drawn.

"What's happening?" I scream to Cristiano. It's loud out here, sirens blaring, people screaming, the blades of a chopper not too far away.

"Straight to the island. Go. Get her out of here,"

Cristiano yells to Alec and turns to run back into that room where it sounds like war has broken out.

"Cristiano!" I break free of Alec and grab Cristiano's arm. His hand is pressed to his side.

He stops, turns back, looking at me for an instant, only it feels like an eternity. "Go. Get out of here."

Alec takes hold of me again and pulls me away from Cristiano. His expression is unreadable as he disappears back into that building. More gunshots ring out, automatic weapons keeping a cadence. The glimpse I have just before the door closes behind Cristiano and I'm carried away, is that of a battlefield. A blood bath.

21

SCARLETT

I take a sip of tea that's gone cold. The same cup Lenore gave me hours ago. I wonder where she is now. She's worried about him. I saw it on her face.

I didn't know she was Alec's aunt. When Alec and our small party got back to the island, I saw that he had caught a bullet, but it was a flesh wound. Still, seeing it, seeing her peel the shirt off his bloody skin and watching his face, I know it hurt like hell. It may have hurt her as much, from the look on her face.

They'd called a doctor in. She said Cristiano and the other men may need him when they're back. When. Not if.

But before the doctor got to the house—because we had to wait for transport by either boat or chopper—Lenore had cleaned the wound. I just sat there and watched.

Blood doesn't bother me. It's strange, in situations like tonight, I'm just really quiet. Calm even. At least on the outside. I'm not sure, maybe it's that I'm slow to process what's happening, to absorb the shock of it. Even after all this time, it is still shocking to hear gunfire considering I was born into a cartel family.

I see my uncle's face again, the moment his body jerked, and he grabbed hold of me. His eyes had gone wide, filled with fear. But they were also remote. The look before death. Before violent death. Maybe it's a godsend.

A gift. A mercy he didn't deserve.

I didn't see my father killed but I watched my mom as she died. Her eyes looked the same as his.

I swipe my eyes with the heels of my hands and drink another sip of cold tea. I'm sitting on the floor of Cristiano's bedroom leaning against the wall, staring out the open window at the still dark sky. I should close it. It's cold but I don't care. Cerberus is beside me, keeping vigil with me. He's quiet. I wonder if he senses his master may be in trouble.

May be dead.

God.

What if Cristiano dies?

No. I can't think about that. It can't happen.

They wouldn't let me bring Noah upstairs. Only

let me down to see him when I screamed bloody murder. What if someone had gotten to him? He's an easy target in that cell. But he was all right. Calmer than me when the guards dragged me back upstairs.

What will happen to us if Cristiano dies?

Just then the sound of the chopper's blades cut through the night. I'm up so fast I tip the cup in my hand, spilling tea on the carpet. Cerberus gives an anxious yelp, his tail wagging once. He remains beside me as I get to the window. The helicopter angles toward the roof, blowing my hair in my face.

I go to the door, Cerberus at my heels. Alec is dozing on a chair outside my door. I don't know why he wouldn't just go to bed. I wasn't going anywhere. He stirs awake when he hears me.

"The chopper," I say.

He's on his feet in an instant and I follow him in the opposite direction from the stairs. We take several turns and climb two sets of stairs. All I can think is, please don't be dead. Please don't be dead. Please God don't let him be dead.

And then before I even see him, I hear him.

"I'm fine," Cristiano growls to someone in his usual annoyed way and relief floods through me.

I'm grateful for Cerberus's bark as he rushes Cristiano coming around the corner. I have a chance to school my features, tamp down my obvious relief.

He's my enemy.

He. Is. My. Enemy. I have to remember this.

He may be the lesser of all the evils but that's only because he needs me. For the moment at least. I know how the cartel works. I understood why my brothers were anxious to get me and Marcus married.

And my uncle's words from earlier ring in my ears.

Cristiano straightens from his crouch where he was petting Cerberus. I see the pain this causes on his face, and I see how he's holding his arm against his side. The blood that stains his tuxedo shirt is obvious. He'd had his hand pressed there earlier too. I remember when he'd missed a step as he'd crouched around me, protecting me. Was that when he was hit? Did he save me from a bullet only to take it himself?

His jacket is gone. He looked nice tonight. Cleaned up.

Then his eyes meet mine and I feel a rush of something I can't or won't name surge through me.

He's using you. Just like every one of them. That's all.

"Cristiano," Dante says as Cristiano comes to me.

Dante got to the house about an hour ago and has left me alone in Cristiano's room. That surprised me but I also saw the worry in his eyes. The near panic. He loves his brother.

"Slow down, man. You've lost a lot of blood," Dante says.

"I'm fine," Cristiano grumbles, stopping in front of me.

He reaches out to touch my face with his good arm, just staring at me for a long minute, thumb caressing my cheek. And I realize I'm doing the same. Staring at him. He blinks, slides his hand to my neck, my arm. He looks me over. "The blood—"

"It's not mine. I'm not hurt," I say quickly.

He nods, looks relieved.

From beside him I see Dante's expression harden in my periphery.

Cristiano grits his teeth, and I can tell he's in tremendous pain. His face drains of color and he closes his hand over my shoulder. In the next moment, I feel his weight.

"Help!" I cry out as he stumbles into me. I reach out to catch him as if I could keep him upright.

Dante grabs hold of him.

"I'm fine," Cristiano grits out, straightening, shoving Dante off. His face contorts as he manages the pain.

"Cristiano!" It's Lenore. She rushes toward him from the top of the stairs, looks him over and then over to Antonio. "Get him to his room. Doctor Marino is waiting."

I'm forgotten in the chaos and watch them go, watch more men shuffle down from the roof. They all look like they've been through a war.

"Come on," Alec says to me.

I turn to find him waiting at the door we just came through. I nod and follow him back down to Cristiano's bedroom where I watch Antonio and Dante ease him onto the bed. The doctor who'd come earlier tears Cristiano's shirt open.

"Get the dog out," Dante orders. "And the girl."

"I'm staying."

"Get her out," he tells Alec.

"She stays," Cristiano says, voice low, but the authority in it no different than if he had roared.

I raise my chin, give Dante a defiant look before nearing the bed to see the damage.

The doctor brings a needle toward Cristiano's arm.

"No," Cristiano says, giving a shake of his head.

"For the pain."

"No. Get the bullet out. Sew me up. I need to get up."

"I also need to reset your shoulder. Again. You're not getting up," the doctor says, putting the needle away, muttering something about how he's always been stubborn.

I laugh. I can't help it. It's the adrenaline leaving my system. Cristiano meets my eyes and opens the palm of his good hand.

"Come here."

I go to him. He looks me over while I watch the doctor cut away what's left of his other sleeve. He's bleeding from his side and his arm lays at a strange angle.

"Why didn't you clean up?" Cristiano asks me.

I look down at myself. "I don't know."

"I'll reset your shoulder first. It's going to hurt but maybe it'll teach you a lesson," the doctor says. "Although I doubt it."

Cristiano smiles and I wonder how much effort it takes him to do that. "For what I pay you, you could pretend to be nice."

"You should pay me double for the number of times I've sewn you back together for Christ's sake."

The doctor looks at me, gives me an expression as if asking if I'm ready.

I bend down, turn Cristiano's face to mine. "You're going to look like Frankenstein soon."

Cristiano grins, opens his mouth to say something and I know the instant the doctor slips his shoulder back into place. I see it on Cristiano's face, see it in how he grits his teeth and hear it in the curse he mutters sending the doctor straight to hell.

"There," the doctor says.

Cristiano turns to him. "I was starting to think you'd forgotten how to do it," he teases. I have no idea how he has the energy. He looks half-dead.

"I've had to reset this shoulder what, three times now?" The doctor tells me, that last part directed to Cristiano.

"Four. You're getting old." Cristiano's eyes flutter closed.

"What's happening?" I ask, panicked.

"Shock. Don't worry, he'll be fine. He's healthy as that monster dog he's got out there."

As if Cerberus has heard and understood, he howls from out in the hallway.

"I need to get the bullet out and clean him up, see what else I need to sew back together. You can go get some rest." He looks me over. "Shower first, maybe."

"I'll stay."

"Go," Dante says to me and I wonder where he was. He's the only one who doesn't look like he's come from battle. "I'll stay with him until the doctor finishes."

"I can—"

"Just go, Scarlett," he grits out. The way he says my name, it's not as hateful as when we've talked before. "I'll stay with my brother." No, not hateful. He sounds defeated.

I rub my face, nod, and walk out of the bedroom to find Alec in his chair and Cerberus anxiously half-sitting staring at the door.

"He'll be fine," I tell them both, petting Cerberus.

Alec nods, relieved.

"Was it Rinaldi?" I ask him. Or the cartel. I don't ask that part.

"Not sure." But I get the feeling he knows something.

"I'm going to shower. I'm just in here." I point to Elizabeth's room. "I promise not to go anywhere so just get some rest or something. You look like shit, Alec."

"I'll be here."

Stubborn as Cristiano.

"Suit yourself." I walk into my borrowed bedroom feeling like an intruder in this little girl's room. A dead girl's room. Killed when she was young enough to play princess.

I think about Noah down in that cell. At least he's alive.

I rub my face and close the door behind me. I'm dead tired but I need to shower and get my uncle's crusted blood off me before I lay down. And what I need to focus on now is getting Noah out of that cell. Whether it was the cartel or Rinaldi, it won't be the last time and if Cristiano doesn't survive the next attack, then Noah's as good as dead locked in that cell.

22

CRISTIANO

"Hey, Brother," Dante says when I open my eyes.

He looks older than twenty-six. Already has gray at his temples. He's too fucking young to have gray around his temples.

"You look like I feel," I say.

"I should have been there."

"So you could get shot up too?"

"So I could fight alongside you."

"Fuck that. I'm glad you weren't there."

"I'm glad you're alive."

"I'm not going anywhere yet, Brother."

"You can't control that," he says, running a hand through his hair.

I can. To some extent. Guilt gnaws at me, but I shove it away. "Did you get the problem solved?"

"What? Oh. Yeah. It was nothing, really. Some stupid emails crossed and just nothing."

"I'm glad Uncle David sent you, Dante. It's better if you're outside of this. Like he is. It's safer."

"I'm not a coward, Brother."

"I know that. But I don't want you in harm's way. This isn't the end. It's not even the fucking middle. And I've been thinking about this. I want you out."

He stands, shakes his head and goes to close the window which is open a crack. "You're either high or delirious."

"I'm neither. I watched them die, Dante. I don't want to watch you die."

"And I don't want to watch you die. So what do you suggest? We both walk away? Fuck that. Fuck Rinaldi. Fuck the cartel. They're not getting away with our family's murders."

I breathe in a long breath, watch my younger brother in the shadowy light of the moon.

"After, then. You're out."

"Let's get to after. You need to get some rest."

I feel myself drift. He's right.

"After," I say again.

"Sure, Brother," he says, and I hear him chuckle as my eyes close.

I DON'T KNOW HOW MUCH LATER IT IS WHEN, AFTER pulling on a pair of jeans, I open the door to my sister's room. I don't like coming in here. Every time I do, I think about how young she was. Just a little girl.

I can't wrap my brain around how anyone could have killed a little girl.

But what happened to Mara? Is it worse?

No. Alive is always better than dead. *If* she's alive. They could have dumped her body in the ocean for all I know but that doesn't feel right. They left a bloody mess behind. It was to make a point. Why go to the trouble of hiding one body?

Mara was sweet. I still remember how she'd always go to Dante when she scraped a knee or fell off a swing. For anything at all, really. Always trying not to cry. Always trying to act like she was older around him.

I'd watch him with her, too, my cool brother. Made fun of him for days after at how he was with her. So careful. So caring.

Moonlight drapes Scarlett in white light. She looks almost otherworldly if I look at her like this. She's lying on her side on the single bed with the Princess pattern blanket pulled up to her shoulders. Her hair has half come out of its braid and is splayed over the pillow.

She mutters something when I stand over her, rolling onto her back, but her eyes don't open. She settles quickly back into sleep. I study her face, free of makeup and dried blood, lips parted slightly to show a neat row of white teeth. Like this, relaxed as she is, she looks younger even than twenty-two.

My fingers play with the hair on Cerberus's head. He followed me in. Since the moment I got up and he saw I was fine, he's come to stand guard just outside her door. It's strange. Cerberus hates people as much as I do. It's one of the reasons I chose him. But he will protect her.

I cross the room to her bed and touch her forehead, brush hair back from her face. It's the only place I see any evidence of what happened. A bruise, small, but there, turning a soft shade of purple. She must have hit her head when I tackled her. I think she'd been in shock standing there, watching her uncle on the floor. An easy target.

I wonder if her uncle knows he saved her life tonight. Not that he'd have done it willingly given the choice of his for hers.

She blinks her eyes open once, twice. Once they adjust to the light and she realizes where she is, she runs the back of her hand over her mouth then her hair and sits up.

I notice she's wearing one of my button-down shirts. The clothes from our shopping trip haven't been unpacked yet. The bags line the hallway outside. I haven't decided where to put them. Where to put her.

"What time is it?" she asks, adjusting the blanket when she realizes one thigh is exposed.

"Late. Or early, depending." I move to sit and wince at the pain in my side. "Are you all right?"

She nods. "Are you?"

I shrug my shoulder, catch myself too late. "Fine."

"Did you take that bullet when you were protecting me?"

"Doesn't matter."

"It matters to me. I wasn't sure but...did you?"

"I don't know, Scarlett," I lie. I did take it when I was trying to get her out of there. "Doesn't matter. We're both alive."

She studies me but drops it. "What happened? Who was it?"

"Cartel. Rinaldi. Both."

"You don't know?"

"We killed some from both crews. Captured a few alive."

"It wouldn't be the cartel. Why would it be the cartel? They killed my uncle."

"No, Little Kitten. You're not that lucky."

"What do you mean?"

"I mean that cockroach will crawl out of his hole yet again."

"He's alive? I thought...I saw him though. I saw him go down."

"He's alive."

She processes, her forehead creased, then continues. "It's not the cartel, Cristiano. Why would they try to kill him? He's one of them."

"It wasn't a bullet that hit him."

"What? What was it?"

"A tranquilizer. Granted it did some damage going in. He must have moved in front of you just in time. I'm pretty sure it was meant for you."

She shakes her head, forehead wrinkling in confusion. "No way it was the cartel. It's still my family." She stops at that and a moment later looks up at me.

"Well, lucky for you they didn't seem to be the most organized crew. There were plenty of them, but the operation was a clusterfuck."

"I thought the plan was for the cartel to work with you."

"Yeah, well, take me out and the cartel is rid of their problem."

"What do you mean?"

"It's more profitable for them to work with Rinaldi."

"Because he's willing to make slaves of women."

I nod. "I can't assume it was Rinaldi, at least he couldn't have done it alone." Something about the whole thing doesn't feel right, actually.

"What do you mean?"

"His family is weakened here. He wouldn't stand a chance against me here or in Naples. Not now. It doesn't make sense that he'd come back and have the manpower to attack alone. He simply doesn't have it."

"So, you think he's working with my family? And you think that tranquilizer was to kidnap me?"

"I don't know. It'd make sense, I guess. He marries you, there's a link between the cartel and his family, but I don't know."

"But why?" I watch her as she says the words. "I mean, I'm not that valuable to the cartel. How can I be?"

"It will mean something to those who were loyal to your father. You're valuable to them. Before, the cartel needed Rinaldi. Needed his connections. Now, Rinaldi needs them more than they need him. He'd need to get you back first thing. It's what would pave the way for a union. Then they could attack me. Take me out. Together and with you back, ensuring the loyalty of those who'd walked away when your father was killed, they'd have the manpower to do it."

"For money. All this just for money."

"Money is a powerful motivator. Almost as much as love."

"As much as hate you mean," she mutters.

"Love is the most powerful."

She looks up at me like she's surprised by that. Then her glance drops to my side. "You're bleeding."

I look down too and sure enough, the white T-shirt I put on has a splotch of dark red where the bandage is. I lift my shirt and look.

Doctor's downstairs eating and he'll be pissed I'm up. I'd get Lenore but she'll mother me too. Dante feels guilty enough not to bother him with this. "Does blood make you queasy?"

She shakes her head.

"Come with me." I stand and wait for her to pull the covers back. She gets up, her feet bare on the carpet, the chipped polish on her toes matching the soft lilac all over this room. "She loved purple, as you can probably guess." I walk into the hallway and Scarlett follows me.

"Elizabeth?"

I nod, enter my room and pull my shirt off over my head with my good arm. I drop it on the bed and turn to find her staring at my back.

"Frankenstein?" I ask.

"It's not that bad," she says, schooling her features.

"You're a bad liar."

"All right. A little like Frankenstein. I'm glad you're not dead."

I feel my eyebrows rise high on my forehead. "Why?"

"Because I think it would mean Noah and I are dead. Or at least Noah is, if you are."

"And here I thought you were concerned for me," I say lightly. I didn't, did I? I sit on my bed, lie back against the headboard and peel off the bandage. I'd do it myself but with my shoulder, it makes it tough.

"Let me help," she says and comes over.

"You don't have a sadistic side, do you?"

She shrugs, looks at the stitches and makes a face.

"Looks worse than it is. Put some of that ointment on it then you can bandage it again and we can get on with things."

"Get on with things," she says, walking into the bathroom. I hear the water go on and a moment later she's back drying her hands. "What sort of things?" She picks up the ointment, reads the label and gives me a grin. "This is going to sting."

"It's going to sting like a mother fucker but you're going to do it."

"Oh, I never said I wasn't," she smiles wide and makes a move so unexpected, it takes me by surprise. She climbs up on the bed and straddles me.

"Don't move."

Fuck. Me.

She squeezes a generous amount of ointment onto her fingers and extends her arm to my side. I grab hold of her wrist before she touches me. "Gentle. Understand? You look like you're going to enjoy this too much for my liking."

"What's the matter, Cristiano? Afraid of a little pain?"

"You just told me you were glad I didn't die," I say, loosening my hold but not letting her go, bracing myself because this is definitely going to hurt.

But I owe her this. I glance to the nightstand where the ring box sits.

I hiss when she smears the stuff on the too tender skin.

She meets my gaze and holds it as she smears it on a little harder than she needs to.

"Take it easy."

Her smile widens at my discomfort. "Aww. What is it?" She tilts her head, pouts, eyes going all big. "The big bad wolf is just a helpless little pup when it hurts?"

I grin. She's sparring, my Little Kitten. That's good. I reach up with my good hand to take hold of the hair at the back of her head. It's pretty much fallen out of its braid and still damp from her shower.

"You like this, don't you, Little Kitten? Me at your mercy?" I squeeze my hand in her hair when she pushes her fingers against the stiches.

"I do like it," she says, her eyes narrowed, almost glowing in the moonlight.

"You're very pretty, Scarlett." I pull her a little closer. "And you know what else?"

"What?" she asks, her confidence melting just a little.

"Your sadistic side is getting my dick hard."

Her hand stops moving and she blinks a few times, realizing what it is she's straddling. I try not to laugh, but it just pisses her off that much more when she sees my attempt to hide my amusement.

"Fuck you! Do it yourself!" She starts to climb off me, but I tug her back.

"All right. Sorry. I'll stop."

Her eyes narrow and she sets her other hand on my bad shoulder. "You think you'll still be hard when I dislocate your shoulder again?"

"Truce. I'm just having some fun. It's been a long time since I've had fun."

"I'm not sure this is the time." She settles back down and focuses on smearing ointment again.

It's quiet for a long moment while I just watch her. She is concentrating, thinking.

"My uncle said something." She only glances at me momentarily when she says it.

"Are you wearing underwear, Scarlett?" I ask, not wanting to talk about her uncle.

Her eyes flash up to mine then away. "None of your business."

I glance down to the exposed skin of her shoulder, the swell of one breast. My shirt is so big on her that it has slid down her shoulder. The way she's got herself situated to avoid my dick, another inch and her pussy will be eye level.

I look at her eyes again. A deep caramel when

she's aroused. And she is aroused. I see it in the way her nipples poke against the shirt. Smell it in the musk between us. And see it in her eyes.

I pull her closer and I don't care that when she resists, she leans her slight weight into my wound. I want her mouth more than I care about the pain.

"Don't you want to know what my uncle told me?" she asks when her mouth is an inch from mine.

"Not really," I say, pulling her to me, kissing her.

"I'll bite," she threatens, the words muffled when I don't let her pull away.

I draw back a little just so she sees me. "I hope you'll do more than that, Little Kitten." I kiss her again, prying her lips open, and, true to her word, sharp little teeth pierce my lower lip. I taste the copper of blood and moan against her mouth. Squeezing her wrist and shifting our position, I topple her onto the bed and pin her down with my weight, trapping one of her arms to the side and taking the pain of her fingernails on the other as they dig into my shoulder.

"You'll open the stitches," she says, scratching her nails down my back.

I groan, pressing my dick against her. "And I just answered my own question. You're not wearing underwear."

She tries to shove at me. "When your men were flying me out of a war zone, we didn't think to stop to pick up our shopping bags, so I didn't have any. Don't kiss me again. I'll bite hard enough you'll need stitches on your lips."

"It'll be worth it," I say, pulling back when her teeth snap at me again. I watch her mouth open and close, watch her pupils dilate when I grind against her clit.

"Stop," she tries.

"There's something dark about you, Scarlett. Something reckless."

She stares up at me, her hips moving a little. I wonder if it's conscious.

"You make me want like no other woman has ever made me want." I dip my head, kiss her neck, feeling her pulse against my lips. Her heart's going a hundred miles a minute.

"Let me go," she says, voice quavering.

"Kiss me and I'll let you go."

She shakes her head. "You already kissed me. Now let me go."

"No. I want *you* to kiss *me*. I want to feel you want it."

She blinks rapidly, looking beyond me momentarily before shifting her gaze back to mine.

"You want to, Little Kitten." I lean close to her ear. "I smell your want."

She flushes at that, but she doesn't deny it.

"Kiss me once. Just once."

"That's all you want? Just a kiss?"

"With tongue." I grin.

"No tongue."

"Just the tip."

She furrows her eyebrows but there's a little lightness beneath all of this resistance. At least for a moment.

"Promise?"

The way she says it gives me pause. The way her eyes glisten. I remember what her uncle told me. "I promise I won't take anything you don't give."

She studies me, considering. She licks her lips, raises her head and brings her mouth to mine. Then she surprises me again when she sweeps her tongue over my mouth before slipping it inside.

I touch it with mine, taste her and when I suck on her tongue, she lets out a little moan. I cup the back of her head then, taking over the kiss, an urgency building as I taste her. I can feel her yield, open. Feel her kiss me back.

I'm hard. Does she feel me?

Reaching one hand between us, I undo the top two buttons of the shirt she's wearing.

She makes a sound, but I swallow it and she doesn't resist when I push it open. Lifting my head slightly to look at her, I cup one breast before undoing the rest of the buttons.

"Cristiano," she mutters when I open the shirt and kneel to look at her bare skin. She has small breasts, a flat belly and a mound of neatly trimmed dark hair between her legs.

I meet her eyes again, lean down to kiss her mouth, her neck, the hollow between her collarbones.

She cups the back of my head, fingers intertwining with hair as I kiss the space between her breasts, then taste her nipple with the flick of my tongue.

"Cristiano." Her fingers curl in my hair pulling a little.

I stop. Like I promised. I rest my cheek on her belly and trace a pattern on it. "You make me want things I don't remember wanting," I say. The urgency fades, something else, something sadder creeping in. I can't allow for that though. Not now.

I kneel again, close the shirt and do the buttons like she had them. I don't want to. What I want is to hold her. To feel her skin against my skin. What I want is more.

She lays her head back on my bed and takes a ragged breath in, watching me. I wonder if she was unsure if I'd stop.

I slide off her, standing. I don't want to, but she needs to learn she can trust me to keep my word. I get the feeling she hasn't had many trustworthy men in her life.

"That wasn't too bad, was it?" I ask, finishing with the last button.

"It was horrible." She sits up.

I grin, close one hand around her thigh to stop her from standing. "Was it? Are you sure about that or are you lying, Little Kitten?"

"I'm not lying."

"So, if I were to spread your legs and look at your pussy, it wouldn't be wet?"

She tries to pull my arm off, focusing all her attention on it.

"Tell me. Tell me again how horrible it was, and I'll have a look."

"Fine. It wasn't horrible, okay?"

I smile. "Okay." I look down at the stitched area at my side. The bleeding has stopped so I hand her a bandage. "Here."

"You need more ointment."

"Fuck no."

"Fine." She peels the paper off the sticky edges and lays the bandage on my side, then looks up at me. "Is it true?"

"Is what true?" I walk to the dresser and open a drawer to get a fresh T-shirt.

"My uncle said something just before the chaos began."

I pull the shirt on and turn to her waiting for her to continue.

"Are you going to make me marry you so the cartel is forced to work with you and not Rinaldi?"

Asshole Jacob.

I study her, try to get a feel for where her head is. Although I can guess. She's about to be told that yes, she will be forced to marry a man she hates. Or should hate.

"Better than Marcus Rinaldi forcing you to marry him, isn't it?"

"They'll still kill you if they can."

"I have no doubt they'll try."

She slips off the bed and comes toward me, then stops, folds her arms across her chest.

"No."

"No what?"

"I'm not doing it."

"I'm hungry. Let's go get some food."

"Did you hear me?"

I open the door and look at her. "I heard you fine and yes, you are doing it. Let's go."

"No."

I sigh, close the door and go to her. She doesn't move away, and I grasp her arms, rubbing up and down, then close my hands and squeeze just a little.

"I understand the circumstances you're coming from, but you need to think now, Scarlett."

"I am thinking."

"What are your options?"

"You can let me go. That's an option."

"Let me rephrase. What are your realistic options? Sit down." I don't wait for her but walk her backward and sit her on the edge of the bed. "The way I see it, you have two and both roads lead to the altar."

"Is this all I'm ever going to be? A pawn for men's games?"

"This isn't a game. Not even close. You marry Rinaldi and you become a party to the flesh trade, not to mention drugs and probably in time, arms dealing. If you stay alive long enough, that is. And that's not even taking Noah into consideration."

"Leave my brother out of it."

"I wish I could."

"You may not deal in flesh, but those other things are just as bad, Cristiano."

"Yeah, but here's the catch." I have never said what I'm about to say out loud. Not to anyone. Not my uncle or brother or Charlie. Not even to myself. "I don't care about it. Not any of it."

Something must change on my face because her expression shifts. Becomes confused then almost worried.

"What do you mean?" she asks more quietly.

I decide I can't say it now, either. Shaking my head, I pick up the box on the nightstand that contains the engagement ring. I open it and look down at it.

"I mean I just want Rinaldi. That's it. I want to know what he said to my mother after he—" I break off. I can't say the words. "And then I want to kill him." That's what I want. It's the reason I survived. And it's all I have been living for.

I turn the box around to show her, but it takes her a very long moment to drag her shiny eyes from mine to the ring. She spares it a quick glance. If she's impressed, she doesn't let on. But she's not the type to be impressed by something like this.

"What happens to you after?"

Smart girl.

"That doesn't matter. You'll be free. I'll make sure you're taken care of, financially I mean, and any other way I can to help you disappear if that's what you want or need. You and Noah both."

"But you said he'd be a soldier."

"You're both mine until this is done. When it's done, when I know what Rinaldi said to my mother and when I've killed him, then and only then are you free."

23

SCARLETT

I study him. He's got a cut high on his cheek but it's nothing compared to his chest and back. He looks like he rolled around in shards of broken glass.

I remember my panic when he'd passed out after the doctor reset his shoulder. I remember exactly how it felt like my heart stopped for a moment. I try to tell myself it's just because if he died, it'd be worse for Noah and me. But I know that's not the whole truth.

"Scarlett?"

He gestures to the ring. It's beautiful, a Princess cut diamond set amidst jagged blue stones.

"Sapphires?" I ask.

He nods.

I study the jewels. Remember how my brothers

had plans to deal in diamonds too. Nothing was off the table for them.

I know I don't really have a choice in the matter here. He is right. This is a better option than Marcus Rinaldi would offer me. But if I have any room to negotiate, I'm taking it.

"I want Noah upstairs tonight. No, now."

"Tomorrow. After you've said I do."

"Tomorrow? This is happening tomorrow?"

"We'll surprise Noah with our happy news."

"We're getting married tomorrow?"

"Problem? Time is of the essence."

"No. No problem." I mean, what does it matter. If Marcus and my brothers had had their way, I'd already be married.

"Good. Anything else?"

"No sex. I sleep in—"

"You'll sleep in my bed and we will consummate the marriage."

"I want my own room and no on the last part."

"You can have your own room, but you will sleep in my bed and the consummation of the marriage is non-negotiable."

"Why? We can just say we consummated the marriage, it's not the middle ages. No one will check for blood on the sheets."

"No."

"What? You're not comfortable lying? Please."

"No, actually. I'm not." He takes the ring out of its box and palms it. Then he traps me. He leans his weight on his fists on either side of me, face so close I'm breathing him in, and the scruff of his five o'clock shadow scratches my cheek. "Besides, all I can think about is how you'll taste when I lick your pussy. How you'll feel when I sink my cock inside you."

"Jesus." I turn away, my heart racing. I find it hard to breathe when he's so close like this. Same when, just a little while ago, I felt him beneath me.

It was stupid to straddle him. That was my bad. I meant to keep him from moving while I rubbed in that ointment I knew would sting like hell.

But he turned the tables on me, didn't he? I get the feeling Cristiano Grigori will always turn the tables on me.

I put my hands on his broad chest, feel the hard muscle beneath warm skin. Feel his heart beat against my palm and remember what it felt like to lie beneath him, all his weight on me. His hard cock between my legs.

Butterflies flutter their wings inside my belly, and I can't help but feel the skin of his chest, touch the scars, press against the hard muscle. Even bruised and cut and stitched, he's a powerhouse. Formidable.

He could be safe for me. For Noah. He could protect us. He took a bullet for me that probably saved my life last night.

But I can't pretend this is good when it is all forced on me.

Shaking my head to clear away stupidity and a naïve desire to want this, I push against him, but he doesn't budge. Only when I stop pushing does he step away. I guess he wants me to know this is on his terms. That everything will be on his terms.

I already know that, though.

He takes the ring between thumb and forefinger raising only his eyebrows at me.

"If I say no, you'll drag me to the altar?"

"Probably."'

"And then what?"

His jaw tightens, his eyes narrow. "Yes or no, Scarlett? I'm getting tired of this conversation. How are we doing this?"

"Sex once. To consummate. Period."

He watches me, blinks, expression steady and unwavering. "How are we doing this?"

He's not negotiating.

But I hold out my hand anyway, turn the palm up to take the ring because we both know I'll agree. It's the only option.

He shakes his head, takes my left hand and pulls me up to stand instead. He slides the ring on my finger like we're a real couple. Like he's my boyfriend and he just proposed, and I said yes, and I'm over the fucking moon.

"Perfect fit," he says.

I look at the ring on my finger. I'm not naïve enough to think this is in any way romantic. Cristiano may be a better man than Marcus, but he's still using me. And I have to keep my eyes on my goal. Get Noah and myself out alive.

"It's worth a lot of money," he says. "And it's yours as long as you do as you promise by accepting it. Just remember one thing," he starts, intertwining our fingers on both of my hands, before drawing them behind my back to hold them in one of his. He squeezes my wrists and tilts my face up by the chin. "We've both made a promise now, you and me. I'm trusting you. You're trusting me. If you betray me, you will make me your enemy. Do you understand that?"

A shudder runs through me.

"You don't need to be afraid of me as long as you don't betray me, Scarlett."

"I'm not afraid of you. Not anymore."

"Hm." He heard my lie but he's distracted. I realize why a moment later when he releases me to take his phone out of his pocket. It must be a text because he doesn't put it to his ear but swipes the screen instead. Whatever he sees makes his eyes narrow, his jaw tense.

"What is it?" I ask.

He types something, the line between his eyebrows growing deeper as he does, then returns his gaze to me as he pockets the phone.

I swallow, his electric blue eyes too intense, too intent on me.

"Do you understand me, Scarlett?" he asks, picking up our conversation like we weren't just interrupted.

I nod.

Because if there's one thing I understand clearly, it's that I do not want to make an enemy of this man.

24

SCARLETT

He left me to eat alone after that strange proposal—can you call that a proposal? It surprised me and although Lenore took a tray into his study, I saw her return with it untouched before I went upstairs.

I look at my ring now as I sit on the little Princess bed. It's pretty, the edges of the sapphires jagged and sharp like shards of glass. I like it. It fits. But the thought of marrying him makes my belly go funny. And it's not exactly a queasy feeling.

Getting up, I pace the room for the hundredth time. I won't be getting any sleep tonight, although it's well past two in the morning. He hasn't come up either but for all I know he's not even on the island anymore. I heard a boat go out a few hours ago. Maybe he went back to the mainland.

I open my door quietly. Still no guard outside.

There's a lock on the outside but he hasn't used it. Yet.

I'm wearing a pair of sweats and an oversized hoodie, along with a pair of ballerina slippers. I added these and a few others like it to the order at the last shop. No way Cristiano would have approved of such a slovenly outfit considering the other pieces he chose for me but I love it.

The soft-soled slip-on shoes are exactly what I need. Quiet.

I put the little plastic flashlight I found in the bedroom into my pocket and make my way toward the stairs. The lights are out apart from a glow that comes from the dining room. Moonlight. I watched its reflection on the water through the huge windows earlier. It was better than watching TV as I ate dinner alone.

Taking hold of the railing, I make my way down the stairs, grateful for the stone. Wood would creak.

Once I'm on the first-floor landing, I look around, making sure I am truly alone. I tiptoe toward the door that leads to the cells below ground.

Strange to think that it was just a few days ago that I was down there. That I watched my brothers' brains blown out.

Poor Noah is still down there all alone. He must be scared. At least after tomorrow he'll be allowed to come above ground.

A soft sound captures my attention before I get

to that dark hallway though. It's coming from Cristiano's study at the end of the corridor.

I take a few steps toward the sound. It sounds like a light buzzing. Like a humming. From beneath his closed door, I see the light on inside. So he's on the island after all. I wonder who took the boat earlier.

I stop then, considering. Would he hear me if I went to Noah's cell? And can I make it back upstairs before he goes to bed? I assume he'll check to make sure I'm in my bed. Would he consider my going to see my imprisoned brother a betrayal?

Shaking my head, I turn back to my original destination.

I agreed. He can give me this. I'm going to say 'I do' no matter what. Plus, Noah is probably still worried about me considering I saw him for all of two seconds the night of the attack and I was covered in blood. Again.

When I get to the corridor, I fumble with the button to switch on the flashlight I dig out of my pocket. I need to give it a good shake, but it blinks twice before casting a dim glow onto my path.

No guards inside. At least not here. I know he's doubled the men outside and on the roof. This house is a fortress.

When I reach the door, I'm grateful to find it unlocked. I hadn't even thought of that. It's the only thing that makes a sound when I open it, whining as I pull it only as far as I need to.

I shine my light on the stairs, but the moment I close the door the flashlight fails altogether, plunging me into utter darkness. A black so complete, it's terrifying. Like being swallowed up by a black hole. Like being the only person left on earth.

Panic has me shaking the flashlight so violently that the little plastic door that keeps the battery in place flies off, sending the battery with it. It makes such a racket as it seems to bounce on every step, that I stand there frozen, holding my breath. I'm sure Cristiano's heard me, maybe Noah did too. He must have.

When the sound stops, I listen but all is silent. I give it one more minute and I try to feel my way down one, two, three steps. But they're too uneven and I'm going to fall and break my neck. I need a flashlight.

Lenore had one in the kitchen. A good one.

I turn back, creep back up the stairs and reach to open the door. I wince at the whine. He wouldn't hear it from the study. He's too far and it's not like a door slamming.

I walk back to the main part of the house and glance down the hall to Cristiano's study. The light is still on, although the sound of the buzzing has stopped. Hurrying, I cross both living and dining rooms to the kitchen and breathe a sigh of relief when I'm inside. Cerberus, laying on his bed in the corner, lifts his head. He wags his tail which thuds against the floor.

"Shh," I tell him with my finger over my lips, but he's excited and probably lonely sleeping in here. I sneak over to him, pet him while imploring him to stay quiet. He licks my face and nuzzles against my ear. It's the sweetest thing. I'm tempted to just curl up with him, but I don't.

Once he's settled, I get up and walk to the drawer where I saw the flashlight. I consider taking one of the sharp knives but decide against it. I have nowhere to keep it and I remember clearly what Cristiano did when he found a simple nail file on me.

Holding the flashlight, I test it. It works and I smile. Petting Cerberus one more time before pushing through the swinging door of the kitchen, feeling a little more self-assured.

But that smile has barely faded when someone grabs me from behind.

I open my mouth to scream but a big hand closes over it and I feel the unmistakable metal of a gun against my ribs. I'm lifted off my feet and carried backward to the wall, the heavy flashlight clanging to the floor. I try to bite the hand clamped tight over my mouth and also find kicking is useless, like kicking a brick wall.

It's Cristiano. Even in the dark I know. Even injured, he's too big, too strong. He's not gentle when he pushes me up against the wall, his forearm at the back of my neck keeping me pinned, the gun brushing my temple.

"I could have killed you," his deep, low voice reverberates against my ear. While my heart is racing, he seems not at all out of breath.

He uncocks the gun. At least I hope that's what the sound is.

My hands are pressed flat to the wall, my cheek smashed against it. I'm having trouble breathing.

As if sensing that, he takes his forearm off me and spins me around. He's keeping me in place, hands on my shoulders, as he looks me over, forehead furrowed, eyes dark.

"What are you doing down here, Scarlett?"

"Did you know it was me when you body slammed me like that into the wall?'"

"Count yourself lucky I didn't shoot first then investigate," he says rather than answering me.

I look at him. He's naked from the waist up and I see blood, just a trace of it, high on the inside of his left arm.

"I asked you a question," he says.

"I—" I look at the gun in his hand and my mouth goes dry.

Shoot first. Jesus. He'd have done that? Is he that

wound up? Am I surprised? He was just attacked at a public event.

He tucks the pistol out of sight into the back of his jeans and looks me over, forehead furrowing. I wonder if that's because of my clothing choice.

"What are you doing down here?" he asks again, meeting my eyes, his a little unfocused.

"I," I start but stop. He's close enough that I smell whiskey on his breath. "Are you drunk?"

He gives me his signature growl. I swear he's part caveman. Then he steps back, stumbling once before turning to glance at me, then away again. He walks back to his study.

"Hey. I asked you a question." I follow him but he's worlds away. When we enter the study, I see the nearly empty bottle of whiskey on his desk.

"You almost killed me. You owe me an answer."

He turns to me, eyebrows raised like he's surprised but there's something else. Something off. He's distracted, like he was earlier when he got that message on his phone.

"I don't owe you anything," he says.

"You pulled a gun on me."

"You're supposed to be in bed. What you doing down here?"

"I wanted to see my brother."

He shakes his head. "You are so fucking stubborn. Do you know that?"

"I've been told a time or two." I fold my arms across my chest.

He looks me over again. "I bought you clothes. Nice clothes. What the fuck is this?"

"You said if I need anything, I should add it to your order."

"I didn't mean this. Don't wear it again. And go to bed. Don't fucking come out of your room again like that. I could have fucking killed you."

"Maybe you shouldn't be walking around with a loaded gun while drunk. If I'm going to have to marry you and live here with you—"

"We're not playing house, Scarlett."

"If I'm going to live here with you," I start again, "We need to get a few things straight. First—"

I never get to finish though. Or even start, really. He's on me so fast I'm still taking a breath in to continue speaking. The door slams shut, and I'm pressed against it, Cristiano against me, one hand in my hair tugging my head back and the other sliding under my hoodie to close around the curve of my hip.

"Do you ever just shut up?" he growls the question into my mouth before he kisses me so hard, all I can do is suck in his whiskey breath and feel his soft lips. "You shouldn't have come down here," he says, kissing me harder, pushing my pants down just far enough that they slip off my hips and pool around my ankles. "You're going to make me do things you don't want me to do."

My eyelids fly open to find his eyes on me as he slips his hand between my legs and cups the crotch of my panties.

I gasp.

We stand there like that for a long minute just staring at each other. My hands rest on his chest but don't push him away. He's about an inch from my face, barely, and he looks fucked up. Not angry. Something else. Just messed up.

"You shouldn't have come down here," he growls again.

"Let me go and I'll go away."

"Too late for that," he pauses, his fingers moving a little. "I haven't had a woman in ten years."

I swallow and push against him, knowing I won't be able to budge him, still not sure I want to.

He moves his hand a little, sliding it up over my panties and to my belly. The pads of his fingers are rough against my skin. My hands curl around his shoulders but I'm not sure if it's to hurt him, to get him off me, or what. But if I'm hurting the shoulder he dislocated, he doesn't seem to care.

"Ten years," he repeats.

He slips his hand into the waistband of my panties and I gasp as his fingers curl into the little mound of hair there, then down. Down to my sex. A sound comes from deep inside his chest. Something animal.

"Cristiano—" I start, his name a breathy whisper.

"And what do I get?" He moves his fingers a little and my mouth falls open to take in a shallow breath. "A virgin."

I swallow hard because his thumb is on my clit and two fingers are smearing my wetness onto me.

"A virgin when what I need is to fuck a whore."

I gasp but when he takes my lower lip between his teeth, I close my eyes and let my head fall back. He releases my lip and kisses my neck, leaving a trail of small bites to my ear.

"I'm going to make you scream," he whispers.

I should stop him. Drag his arm off me. But his fingers are doing something to my clit that feels better than when I do it to myself. His hand is so big, the pads of his fingers rougher than my own fingers, and I'm already soaked. Needy. So needy.

But then he pulls his hand out of my panties and steps back.

I stumble forward on an exhale of air I'd been holding. He catches me, sets his hands on the neck of my hoodie and in an instant, it's off. Ripped in two, sliding off my arms.

"What—"

I look down at the ruined top, then back at him.

He glances down at my breasts which are exposed now. I wasn't wearing a bra. I'm a B-cup on a really, really good day and today isn't one of those days. My first thought—because I'm a dummy—is to wonder if he's disappointed. Although it's not the first time he's seen them, but that time was different. Very different.

I move to cover them, but he takes hold of my hands, bringing my arms to my sides and looks again. It's a moment before he shifts his gaze back to my eyes, my mouth. He smears his fingers across my lips, and I taste myself. I should be outraged. Humiliated.

"Open your mouth."

I swallow.

"I said open your mouth."

I lick my lips and do as he says. He pushes a finger into my mouth.

"Suck."

I do. I have to.

His breathing is ragged, eyes dark. He tastes like me.

"Fuck, Scarlett." He pulls his finger out and kisses me hard. There's something urgent about the kiss. Something possessive and hungry.

"I'm going to devour you," he says, then draws back just a little, eyes on me as he crouches down. Placing one knee on the floor, I watch his dark hair as he peels my panties down, exposing me, taking the time to slide them all the way to the floor. His knuckles whisper along my skin before he helps me step out of them.

I feel exposed and shiver when he pushes two fingers of each hand into my triangle of hair then down to spread my lower lips.

He looks at me for a long, long time. I think about the ten years comment. Has he really not had a woman in that long? Is that normal for men?

"I smell you."

I swallow. I'm wet. I feel it trickling down the inside of my thigh.

"I smell your want."

When he closes his mouth over my clit, I lose the thread of my thoughts, only feeling his warm, wet mouth on me, his tongue licking me. My hands move, one into his hair the other onto his shoulder. He pushes my legs wider and licks and sucks. I'm gasping for breath, moaning, my eyes cast down to watch him. When he takes my clit into his mouth, I'm undone. I come. I come so fucking hard my knees give out and he has to hold me upright as he sucks harder.

I bite down on my own lip, cutting it. I taste that copper of blood and I realize that moaning, growing louder, is mine. Me. Blubbering words, calling for god. Calling *him* god. I don't even know. I just...my god. I've never felt like this before. Never come like this before. I'm bucking with it and all I can feel is him. On me. His hands. His mouth. His tongue. Him.

I'm limp when it's over, a whimper all I have left to give.

He meets my eyes, holding onto me as I slide down to my knees. I stare up at him as he sets his other knee on the floor. His eyes, my god. His eyes. They're so beautiful even for the sadness ever present in that brilliant blue.

I think about what he said. How none of it will matter after he does what he has set out to do.

And I understand what it means and something inside my chest twists at the thought.

I touch his face. When he kisses me, I kiss him back and let him have my tongue.

He wraps a hand in my hair again and draws my head back, kisses my throat, bites the curve of my neck before facing me again.

"Take me out, Scarlett." His voice is a growl.

I lick my lips, looking down at the crotch of his jeans, at the erection pushing against it. I fumble when I reach for him, undoing the button, the zipper, pushing his jeans and briefs down far enough to see him.

He's big. Thick and throbbing, a vein pulsing.

I look up at him and he guides my hand. I close my fist and he squeezes his hand over mine so hard I'm sure it must hurt him.

"Fuck," he starts, and I watch in awe as he pumps his cock once, twice, then stops to pull me close, to kiss me again, his cock at my belly, the tip wet on my skin. He kisses me as he guides himself between my legs and I draw in a breath when he rubs himself over my still-sensitive clit, between my wet folds.

"Oh, god."

He looks at me then. We're so close. All it would take would be the slightest shifting of position and we'd be even closer. He'd be inside me.

I swallow hard, wanting it. Wanting him to do it. Greedy in my desire to be closer. To feel him fill me. Greedy to come again. It's the first time I've wanted a man like this. I never thought I'd want to be touched by a man again.

But then he makes a sound, a low groan followed by a curse. He draws back so abruptly, I startle, and the moment is gone. Poof. Just like that. Like it never even was.

He stands, turning to tuck himself away.

I remain on my knees staring up at him and his look is pained when he looks down at me.

"You need to go upstairs," he says, his tone on edge. Tight.

"Why?"

He looks me over again, shakes his head, walks back to his desk where his shirt carelessly hangs over the back of his chair. He takes it, tosses it to me.

"Get dressed. Go upstairs. Get out of here. Now."

I pull the shirt on, feeling embarrassed. Unwanted.

I stumble to my feet and watch him tilt the bottle back to swallow the rest of the whiskey.

When he turns to me, his eyes are shuttered.

"Noah's already upstairs. You don't go down to the cells again, understand?"

"He is?"

"Do you fucking understand?" he asks, stepping toward me almost aggressively and forcing me to take a step back.

I nod quickly. I'm still afraid of this man. It's a mistake to be anything but afraid. He's holding on to his sanity by a very worn thread.

"What happened just now? I don't understand—"

"Go upstairs, Scarlett. Please," he says through gritted teeth.

I want to. I want to run out of here but he's too close. Beyond him I see the pot of ink on the desk, a towel, what looks to be a homemade tattoo machine. I look at his chest, at his arm where the bloody streak was, and see the dark lettering. I don't know if it's too dark or just badly done, but I can't read it.

He walks to an armoire and opens it, takes out a fresh bottle of whiskey and twists the lid off.

"Haven't you had enough?" I ask.

He turns to me, looking at me as he swallows three glugs out of the bottle. "Go to bed, Scarlett. I mean it. I'm about this close to losing what little control I have left tonight."

"What did you do?" I ask, pointing to the spot. "Did you add a name?"

He steps toward me, the bottle dangling in one hand at his side. "Enemies crawl inside my house the way maggots crawl over a corpse."

Hate punctures his words making the visual that much more terrible. It takes all I have not to back away from him.

"Where the fuck is Alec?" he barks, then opens the door and yells for him. But when he doesn't come, he mutters a curse and loudly sets the bottle down on his desk, some of the whiskey splashing out.

He takes my arm roughly to march me out of his study and to the stairs.

"Let go!"

But he doesn't let go. He drags me and when I stumble, he just keeps going, righting me as we take the stairs. Like he's bringing an errant child up to her room.

"Let me go. You're hurting me!"

"Remember it next time and do as I say," he barks as we get to my borrowed bedroom. He opens the door. "In," he says and deposits me inside.

"What did I do?" I cry out.

He opens his mouth as if to answer then shakes his head closing the door between us. Then, for the first time since he's put me here, he locks me in.

25

CRISTIANO

She's right about the whiskey. I've had enough.

But I walk into my bedroom, slam the door shut and pick up the bottle there to drink some more. Because tonight, I need it.

I place my gun on the nightstand and bring my fingers to my nose to smell her on them. The taste of her mixed with the taste of the whiskey makes me heady.

My dick is still hard. I need to fuck. Maybe I should have fucked those women my uncle supplied all this time. I couldn't touch them though. Turned my stomach to think of it.

Her though? Fucking Scarlett De La Cruz with that big mouth she doesn't know when to shut. Her whiskey eyes and tiny tits. Her pussy smelling like perfume and tasting like the sweetest thing I've ever tasted?

Yeah. I could fuck her.

I could fuck her for days.

I shove my jeans and briefs off and switch on the shower because if I don't do this now, right fucking now and right fucking here, I'm going to go back into that room and fuck her so hard I'll rip her in two.

I meant what I said. I get a virgin when I need a whore. Because I can't take her the way I want to. The way I need to. Not yet.

And so, with the hand I used to finger her I fist my dick and pump so hard it's just this side of pain. When I come, it's with one fist against the wall and the vision of her little pussy in front of my eyes. The neat little triangle of dark hair, swollen little nub poking out at me, for me. Her pussy leaking onto my tongue as she called out my name.

Called me god.

Christ.

Fuck.

I curse her as waves of orgasm take me under, drowning me. Because I am drowning. Life is drowning me.

When it's done, I'm out of breath. Out of energy. I sit on the bench, back against the wall, eyes closed. Water washes over me. I'm too drunk to think. Which is exactly what I wanted tonight. What I needed. Besides her, that is.

She's lucky I had sense enough to lock her away. Never mind that I have the key.

Standing again, I switch the water to cold and suck in a breath with the first icy wave. I make myself stand under it. It's what I need to do. It'll wake me up.

And I need to wake the fuck up.

Because what Charlie sent me today is fucked up. Marcus Rinaldi isn't working alone, and I don't mean the cartel. I've suspected that for years but now I'm sure.

There's no way the cartel would just help him to attack me. Would help him when they know doing so would set me against them. They wouldn't risk losing their inroad to Europe, not now. The Rinaldi family doesn't have enough manpower to stand against me so it makes no sense that the cartel would simply back him.

No. Marcus has had some help.

I touch the spot on my arm where I fumbled the newest name. It's illegible but maybe that's a good thing because it was a stupid thing to do.

Switching off the water, I grab a towel, dry off then discard it and walk into the bedroom naked. I pull back the covers and climb into bed. Lenore changed the sheets so there's no blood, but that means I can't smell her on them anymore either.

That'll all change tomorrow night though, I tell myself.

Come tomorrow night I can have her till my heart's content. I'll go slow. Build it up. Teach her to take what I give the way I give it. Teach her to come when it hurts.

I close my eyes, but sleep doesn't follow. Only the photo Charlie sent. Marcus Rinaldi sitting on a rickety wooden chair in the De La Cruz house drinking from a bottle of tequila. A woman on her knees sucking him off while Felix and a crew of Cartel men stand around probably plotting how they'll off him when he's no longer useful. When they can take over.

Marcus the idiot getting his fucking dick sucked at the exact time that we were attacked here. He's no mastermind behind any plot. He's just not that smart. That attack wasn't him.

I don't sleep much. Haven't in years. But after lying in a coma for six long years, there's time I need to make up for. I wonder if I'll always feel this way.

I roll onto my side and reach to open the night-stand drawer, taking out the stack of photos there. Old photographs of my family. Us when we were little. All of us. My brothers, my parents so young, then a few with my baby sister.

And even as I see myself in those pictures, even as the proof that I was there is right in front of me, is in my fucking hands, I don't feel a thing. Not a mother fucking god damned thing. I can't. Because I can't remember any of it. Not the vacations. Not me on my father's shoulders in the pool. Not my mom hugging me when I fell and scraped my knee.

I don't remember the events and I don't remember my family. My only memory is the night they were killed.

What a cruel thing that that's the one thing that sticks in my stupid brain.

26

CRISTIANO

My head throbs in the too-bright sun as I stand on the beach drinking coffee while Cerberus plays in the waves. I need to make some calls today. Organize our impromptu wedding.

Cerberus runs back to me as wind whips my face. It's a brisk morning. He drops the ball I've been tossing for him at my feet and lays down, ready for more.

"You're quite the guard dog, you know," I tell him, picking up the ball and throwing it into the waves.

He charges after it and I watch. I love that dog. I love his innocence. The honesty of his existence.

My arm aches. It's the same one the doctor reset yesterday. I peel back my shirt to glance at the tattoo. Why I thought I could write a name in script no less at that angle while drunk is honestly beyond me. I shake my head at myself and finish my coffee, unable to resist looking up at her window again.

It's been empty every time, but she's there now, her face turned up to the sun. She has her eyes closed as I watch her.

That tattoo wasn't the only idiotic thing I did last night. I kissed Scarlett. That's twice now I've done it. The rest of it, tasting her, wanting my dick inside her, that I can classify as sex. I don't have to overthink it. But kissing her is so fucking personal. And looking in her eyes when I do it is just fucking stupid.

Cerberus barks.

Her eyes snap open and they lock on mine. She's surprised to see me here, and a moment later, she's gone from sight.

I rub my face, push my fingers into my hair. I've got to get my head on straight. Keep my eye on the goal. On why I'm doing any of this.

Punish those who had a hand in the murders of my family.

Period.

Destroy Marcus Rinaldi.

Period.

Put him in an early grave.

Period.

The end.

If I let myself get caught up in Scarlett De La Cruz and how good she tastes when I kiss her, how she feels and sounds when she comes, it will weaken me. Her uncle saw it last night. Just read it right on my face when I saw her standing there in that dress, looking like she didn't belong here on earth.

The chopper's blades cut into the morning.

I look up at it, see my uncle in profile. I feel nothing at the sight of him. Should I feel something?

Without looking away I whistle for Cerberus who comes running out of the water, standing a little too close to shake off the excess.

"Come on," I tell him as we head to the kitchen door.

"She refused breakfast," Lenore says from the sink, giving me a sideways glance.

"Hunger strike. It's what she does."

She turns off the tap, picks up a towel and turns to me as I lift the espresso pot to pour myself another cup of coffee.

"Why don't you take some coffee up at least."

"I'm not her servant."

"Don't be stubborn," she tells me and shoves a second cup toward me.

"Fine."

She nods, pleased with herself, I guess.

"I'm only doing it because I need to talk to her about the wedding anyway."

"Sure, Cristiano." She doesn't say it sarcastically, but I hear her. Lenore knows me well. Better than anyone else. "Do you want me to show your uncle into the study?"

"No. Keep him here. Put Cerberus with him."

She nods, grins because she knows how much Cerberus likes my uncle. "It's good you're going to ask Father Michael to perform the ceremony. Your parents would be pleased."

Father Michael married my mom and dad too.

Without a reply because I don't know how to reply, I walk out of the kitchen, leaving Cerberus to have his breakfast.

I'm not sure what to expect this morning. That's the thing with her. I never know what to expect. She's unpredictable to the point of being reckless. I'm surprised she survived Marcus considering his temper, but I guess her brothers stood between him and her. Hell, I don't know how she survived them.

I get upstairs to find Alec standing outside her door and the sound of women talking inside. They're speaking in Italian so it's probably the women doing her hair and makeup.

"Where's the brother?"

"End of the hall in one of the guest rooms." The house is coming together slowly, one room at a time.

"Good." Pushing the door open, I stop to take in the scene.

Scarlett's wearing a robe standing with her arms folded across her chest obviously refusing something. She doesn't have a stitch of makeup on and her hair hangs in loose waves down her back. She looks pissed. Again.

"What's the problem?" I ask.

They all turn to me and the women start. Scarlett just watches as they tell me she won't let them do her hair or her makeup.

I turn to her, raise my eyebrows.

"I can brush my own hair and put on my own makeup."

"That's it? You want to do your own hair and makeup?"

She narrows her eyes, juts her chin out, then nods once.

"Fine." I turn to the women, thank them for their time and tell them to leave. Tell them they'll still be paid.

Although irritated, they pack up the few things they'd unpacked and are gone in a few minutes.

I sip my coffee.

Scarlett eyes the second cup.

"Lenore says you won't eat. Is this another hunger strike? Because I thought we talked about how effective they are."

"I remember. You'd have to be of some value for it to work. I know my worth to you, Cristiano."

My jaw tenses. I set her mug on the nightstand. She can drink it or not. I could give a fuck. I need to get this girl out of my head and out of my system.

She's fucking with me. Tonight will do the trick. Fucking her will do it.

"All right. You got what you wanted. We leave at five this evening. Be ready. And fucking eat something for Christ's sake."

"And my brother?"

"Will walk you down the aisle if you like."

She appears surprised.

"If you don't plan on being an idiot about it."

"I'm not an idiot."

"No, you're not but you sure can act like one. Give me your word, Scarlett. Tell me you're not going to give me any trouble."

"Is this all because I told you to stop drinking?"

I take a deep breath in, sip my coffee and count to ten. She is right. I was the idiot last night.

Not to mention being an asshole to her.

"Are you going to give me trouble or do you want your brother there tonight?"

"My brother." She folds her arms across her chest.

"Good."

"Why? Why are you being nice?"

"I'm a nice guy." I give her a smile that's more a baring of teeth than anything else.

"Or is it that you fucked your whore last night like you wanted, and you feel guilty?"

That stops me. "What?"

"I heard the chopper go out. After you dragged me upstairs, I mean."

"And you think I went off the island to find a whore to fuck?" Is she serious?

"Did you?"

"Would you care if I did?"

"I don't want any diseases."

I snort, put my mug down and go to her. "I didn't fuck any whore. I didn't even leave the island. That was two of my men who went to the mainland."

She looks at me, studies my eyes. Maybe she's trying to gauge if I'm telling the truth. Then she shrugs a shoulder like she could care less but I know better.

"I used my hand."

It takes her a moment to catch on and her mouth falls open when she does.

I grin. "I used my hand to jerk myself off. Is that what you wanted to know?"

"More than I needed to know, actually. Spare me the details."

"Virgin ears can't take it?"

"You know what? Fuck you. Our marriage is just a front anyway. You can fuck anyone you want. You don't have to explain anything to me."

She takes a step back, putting space between us, and picks up her mug to sip. That's when I notice she's not wearing the ring.

"Where's your ring?" I ask urgently.

"I took it off last night. After you manhandled me up here and locked me in all for—"

"Where is the fucking ring, Scarlett?"

She looks confused but gestures to the bathroom.

I walk in to find it on the counter by the sink. Picking it up I return to the bedroom to take the mug from her hands, not caring about the splash of scalding coffee on my fingers. I push the ring back on her finger.

"Ow. You don't have to be so rough."

I squeeze her wrist. "Some girls need rough. *You* need rough."

"Why are you so angry with me? What did I even do?"

I close my hands over her shoulders and walk her backward to the wall.

"It doesn't come off again."

"Fine."

"Tonight, you're going to be my wife. That means something to me."

"It shouldn't. It doesn't mean anything to me."

"No? Are you changing your mind?"

She stares up at me. She's testing. "I'm just making sure you know I'm only doing it because I don't have a choice, Cristiano."

I look down at her, at the expanse of skin exposed by the robe. Reaching down I finger the knot of the belt taking my time to undo it. I trace my knuckle over the center of her chest, up over her throat so she tilts her head back a little. I only stop when I have her chin in my grasp. I hold her at an angle that's just short of comfortable.

"I know what they did to you," I say.

She clenches her jaw, narrows her eyes.

"Your brothers. I know what they did when Rinaldi wanted a look."

Pink flushes her cheeks, and her eyes go from indignant, to hurt, to accusing.

"They humiliated you."

Tears well in her eyes but she doesn't look away. Doesn't attempt to pull free.

"While your uncle stood by and watched."

Those tears begin their procession down her cheeks, thick and wet. But she still won't look away. Good. She and I both need to look at things with eyes wide open.

"I could force you, Scarlett. I could humiliate you. Hurt you."

I feel her swallow when she lowers her lashes, letting those tears rush out.

"Isn't that what you're doing?" she asks, voice quieter than usual.

"You don't make this easy, you know that?" I let her go, step back, and run my hand through my hair.

"How did you know?" she asks, her voice tight.

"Your uncle told me."

"Of course, he did. Did he tell you he tried to stop them? Because that would have been a lie."

"I know the kind of man he is."

Silence, then, "What do you want, Cristiano? Why are you here? I'm going to do what you said, what we agreed. So why bother talking to me now after the way you treated me last night?"

"Do you remember what I said last night about my enemies?"

I see from her face she does. It was graphic. Overdone, I admit.

She nods.

"I need a friend, Scarlett. Just one friend."

She studies me, confused. I get it. I'm confused too. Is this what I'd intended to say when I came in here?

She snorts then, shaking her head and wiping errant tears off her cheeks.

"Why do you do this?" she asks.

"Do what?"

"Mess with me. First there's what happened last night. You almost kill me, then you...you kiss me and," she pauses, breaking eye contact and pushing her fingers into her hair. "After you do what you do, you order me out of your study like I'm used up. A piece of trash."

"You're not a piece of trash. I never said that."

"It's how I felt. How you made me feel."

"Well, that wasn't my intention. I was protecting you."

"Protecting me?"

"Yes."

She shakes her head again as if dismissing that. "Then you drag me upstairs practically pulling my arm out of its socket and lock me in here. Then this morning you come in here looking all guilty—"

"Guilty?"

"And manhandle me again, then ask me to be your friend? Are you schizophrenic? Is that what this is?"

I chuckle. I shake my head this time.

"Have you gone off your meds, Cristiano?"

"Be careful, Scarlett."

"Because if you think I'm your friend, you've surely lost your mind."

I fist my hands at my sides, force myself to breathe. This was a mistake. Saying what I just said —god what the fuck even possessed me to say it?

I need to get out of here before I hurt her because man does she know the buttons to push.

"You and me, we're enemies. Enemies to the end," she says, a new energy fueling her words.

"To what end?" My self-control is gone in an instant. Before I can think, I slap my hands to the wall on either side of her head so hard and so loud, I'm sure there's a dent.

She jumps, deer-in-headlights eyes on me. There's only fear in them now.

"You want to be my enemy, Little Kitten?"

I watch her throat work as she swallows.

"You got it. Enemies until the end. Know that you've just made the biggest mistake of your life."

Only when I push off do I hear her audibly exhale.

She wobbles and slides down the wall a little before locking her knees to stay upright.

I fist a handful of hair to make her look at me. "You just make sure you look pretty for me and you say those two little words. Because if you don't, I'll break your brother's neck in front of your eyes and throw his broken body at your feet. Are we clear?"

She stares at me with terror in her eyes. Stares at me like she's looking at the devil incarnate. And maybe she is.

"Are we fucking clear?" I scream and she whimpers, cowering. Cowering away from me. And fuck me.

I release her, slam a fist into the wall.

I hate myself right now. Hate myself because what have I become? What kind of monster am I?

"Ah, fuck you Scarlett! Fuck you for doing this to me!"

SCARLETT

"**F**uck *you for doing this to me.*"

Right.

Because I made him threaten to break my brother's neck. I made him into this crazy man who has a personality disorder.

Who's scary as fuck.

I suck in a shaky breath. He wants me to look pretty tonight? That's not happening. My eyes are puffy and red, skin blotchy from crying all day long and over what? Him? God. Something is seriously wrong with me. Maybe it's me with the mental disorder.

"I need a friend, Scarlett. Just one friend."

I pick at my cuticle and try to forget how he looked when he said that. How he sounded.

How much more screwed up can things get?

Someone knocks on the door and I expect

Lenore with another tray of food. She's tried twice now but it's not that I don't want to eat. It's that I can't.

It's close to five so I guess it's a soldier making sure I'm getting ready. I'll be ready. I won't look pretty but I'll put on a dress and show up and say those two words. Period.

"Come in."

But when the door opens, Noah's standing there looking fresh from the shower, wearing clean clothes and smiling at me.

"Noah!" I hop off the bed and run to him, jump into his arms. I swear he's grown taller just in the last few days.

He hugs me back. "You're going to crush my ribs," he says.

"Oh, God it's so good to see you." An onslaught of tears springs from my eyes.

Alec clears his throat. "Chopper leaves in half an hour. Your brother will bring you to the roof." He looks at Noah who nods.

"What's this? Are you working for him already?" I ask my brother.

Noah doesn't quite meet my eyes.

"Cristiano wants to know if you need anything," Alec says.

"I just need him to go to hell. Can you tell him that for me?"

He clears his throat. "Thirty minutes."

Once the door is closed, Noah walks in a circle, taking in the room. "Have you been living in this lap of luxury while I've been in that cell?" He picks up a plastic toy and cocks his head to the side. "How old does he think you are, like five?"

"It's his sister's room. And he moved the lock to the outside. That's why I'm in here. You agreed to work for him?"

"What choice did I have? And besides, he hasn't been horrible to me. Better than my own brothers, at least."

"Well, shit. Isn't he wonderful then?" I grin sarcastically, probably looking like some maniac. "Because our brothers set the bar pretty damn low, Noah."

"This is our world, Scarlett. It's been our world. You need to stop fighting it and figure out a way you can live inside it."

"I'll never stop fighting him."

"Our family murdered his family. Tried to kill him."

"No, not our family. Diego and Angel. Not us. Not our parents."

"Well, I can see where he's coming from."

I snort.

He sits on the bed, tests it. "Nice. I got a room down the hall but it's pretty bare bones."

"Lucky you. Is your lock on the outside?"

"Stop feeling sorry for yourself. You're alive.

We're alive. He's going to marry you. You'll be his wife."

"For the cartel. He is using me to get to the cartel."

"Doesn't matter. It means something to him."

"How do you know that?"

"Because it's different than it was when it was Rinaldi. I know how Rinaldi was to you."

I feel my face burn. Does he know what they did too? Did our uncle enlighten my kid brother to my humiliations? I scrub my hands over my face but when I open my eyes, I'm still here, in this little girl's room. Still trapped in this nightmare.

"Cristiano, even the way he talks about you is different," Noah goes on and it's like we're living in two different worlds.

"What do you mean when he talks about me?"

"Nothing." He shrugs a shoulder. "When he told me about the wedding and all."

My right hand moves to turn the engagement ring on my finger and my brother looks at it. He comes toward me, takes my hand.

"He gave you that?"

I look at it too and shrug a shoulder. "Please don't tell me you're impressed. A big diamond means nothing."

"It's not that," he says, studying it.

"What is it then?"

"I was just downstairs. You don't know?"

"Know what?"

"It's his mother's ring."

"What?"

"In the portrait in the living room. The one that looks like she's staring right at you."

"I know the portrait but I never noticed a ring."

"I had some time to study it while Cristiano was in a meeting with his uncle. That guy's a dick by the way."

"Well, we agree on that."

I look down at the ring anew and remember how he looked panicked when I had taken it off this morning. Why would he give me his mother's engagement ring?

"See. He's different than that douche, Rinaldi."

I shake my head. "Don't do that. He's not better than Marcus or our brothers," but even as I say it, I know it's not true and his words ring in my ears and I want to shut them out. Shut him out.

"I need a friend, Scarlett. Just one friend."

Crap.

I understand that need. Why did I push him? I know he's hurt. I know he's alone. I think Cerberus is truly his only friend and how sad is that?

"Are you wearing that to your wedding?" Noah asks.

I have to swipe the back of my hand over my eyes to clear away any stray tears before I look down at myself in this oversized robe. "I should. It'd serve him right."

"He hasn't hurt us, Sis. He probably has more right to than anyone else had but he hasn't."

I study my little brother, see him for the fifteen-year-old kid he is. Diego and Angel were the worst to him. Found him weak because he's gentle. Because somehow, in our world, he manages not to be filled with hate.

"I'll get dressed," I say, going into the closet which can swallow up the various rooms I've been locked in whole.

The dress he chose is simple. Just a straight satin floor-length white silk gown that fits like a second skin. I actually like it. But I'm not wearing it. Right beside it is the one that's more fitting.

Once I'm dressed, I walk out and stand in front of the full-length mirror.

"That's the dress?" Noah asks, looking confused. He's holding something in his hand. A toy or something. "I guess it's prettier than what Marcus had you wearing."

"Anything would be prettier than that disaster." I finger comb my hair. I already decided to leave it down and I don't plan on much makeup. Just a little mascara and lipstick.

"One day, when this is all over, you'll actually fall in love."

"No, I won't. Love just isn't in the cards for me." I

say, my throat closing up again. How am I ever going to make it through this ceremony?

"No veil?" Noah asks.

I glance at my mother's veil. "I don't want to get blood on it if things go wrong." It's a joke but in such poor taste even I wince.

"Well, you look really pretty," he says. "Different than you did when it was Marcus."

"Thanks. Hey, you're walking me down the aisle, right?"

"What?" he asks, putting the toy down and picking up a framed photograph.

"You'll walk me down the aisle?'"

"Someone has to or you're going to trip over your own feet in those shoes," he says, pointing to the pair of four-inch pumps that look like Cinderella's glass slippers. He glances at the photo again. "Scarlett, do you know whose room this was?"

I come to glance at the photo of the little girl standing with some friends around a swimming pool, hair soaked, all with happy smiles on their faces. "Elizabeth. Cristiano's sister."

"Elizabeth?"

"Yeah. She was killed, too."

"Do you know this one's name?" he asks, pointing to the little blonde-haired girl next to Elizabeth.

I shake my head.

He turns the photo over and takes it out of the frame.

"Mara," he says before turning it over to study her again.

"She was here too, apparently. She's Lenore's granddaughter. She disappeared. I don't want to think about what they might have done to her."

He nods, puts the photo down but seems preoccupied as he walks me out of the bedroom and down the stairs.

28

CRISTIANO

I check my watch, adjust my cuff link. She has four minutes.

It's cooler today than it's been, a storm rolling in. I watch the clouds as I think about the afternoon. My uncle is pissed I wouldn't tell him where the wedding would take place.

I don't want him there for a stupid reason. I don't want him to see my mother's ring on Scarlett's finger.

Lenore must have mentioned that Father Michael would be performing the ceremony. He thought that was dramatic and unnecessary.

I told him I needed it to be done right. In a church with a priest. No city hall. I told him I didn't want the cartel thinking it's not a real marriage. Not that I really think they would. We'd be legally married in a ceremony at civil hall too.

"The men have secured the chapel, sir," Antonio says to me.

I nod and the roof door opens.

"Still not sure why a justice of the peace wouldn't have done it," Dante notes.

I don't comment. He doesn't like Scarlett simply because she is a De La Cruz. I understand.

Noah steps out first. He's dressed in one of my old suits. It's got to be at least ten years old, but he looks better than he did a few days ago. He smiles and nods to me. He's not a bad kid. I only spent about an hour with him, but no one would believe he was cut from the same cloth as his two older brothers.

Then again, they only share one parent. Scarlett and Noah's mother was Manuel De La Cruz's second wife. He left his first wife, Diego and Angel's mother, for her. I have a feeling that had something to do with the bad blood between them.

I gesture to the pilot that we're ready to go as Noah pushes the door wider and Scarlett steps onto the roof. She's huddled into a heavier coat than I'd expect for the temperature and is hugging it closed.

When she sees me, she quickly averts her gaze.

Lenore steps out after her.

"Thank you, Noah," I say to him as they approach, then turn to Scarlett. "You look nice," I tell her. "As always."

She looks up at me, her lashes thicker for the

mascara accentuating the soft caramel-brown of her eyes.

"You don't look like a Neanderthal," she says.

"Well, that's something."

"I didn't say you weren't one."

I grunt.

She shivers.

"Are you cold?"

She looks around anxiously. Shakes her head.

Once the others are on board, I gesture for her to climb on.

Her expression grows weary at the chopper, the blades whirring overhead growing louder as they kick up the wind.

"It's safe," I tell her and help her in.

"Why can't we just get married here?"

"We need a church." I close the door and when we lift off, Scarlett grips the edges of her seat. I reach over to strap her in.

For the duration of the short flight, no one but Noah speaks. Lenore doesn't much care for the chopper and it's obvious how Scarlett feels. Noah, at least, is excited. Exactly as I'd expect a boy his age to be. He's asking all kinds of questions, eyes bright and exhilarated.

It's a short ride and once we arrive on the mainland, everyone unloads. The SUVs are waiting to take us to the chapel. A small and mostly unknown place in a village just a little too far out of the city to become trampled by tourists.

It's always strange to me how throngs of people can collect in one place. Everyone literally overrunning each other, and call it a vacation. As if crowds are remotely enjoyable. Meanwhile, if they ventured just a mile farther, they'd find undisturbed, quiet beauty.

"Where are we going?" Scarlett asks me as I lead her to one of the SUVs.

"You'll see."

I climb into the SUV beside her and our procession starts its drive along the coast to Santa Elena, a tiny fishing village where Father Michael awaits our arrival at the chapel known to the locals as the Blue Chapel.

Scarlett keeps her gaze on the water. "It's pretty out here."

"It is."

She turns to me. "Why did you give me your mother's ring?"

I'm surprised she knows, but I guess I shouldn't be. One look at my mother's portrait and she'd recognize the ring.

"I don't know," I say. It's an honest answer. I'm tired of going around in circles trying to make sense of things that don't make sense. That's all I seem to run into with her.

"I won't take it. When it's over, I mean. I'll give it

back to you."

"I told you it's yours. I have no use for it."

"It's your mother's ring. Even you have to have more feeling than that."

The words are a blow. "It's yours, Scarlett."

"I'll wear it as long as we're married, but I won't take it from you. It's not right."

We'll see. I don't say it out loud and she shifts her gaze back out the window.

"Are you ever jealous of them?" She gestures to the couples on the beach bundled up against the cool evening, taking in the last of the sun.

"I don't think about it."

"You don't think about a different life?" she asks, looking at me again. "Where you're not you?"

"Do you?"

"What do you think?"

I glance beyond her momentarily, taking in the colors of the sunset on the water before meeting her eyes again. That's when it happens. When I have that brain rattling moment again. When a flash of memory sends a shock of electricity straight through me.

Us on the beach. That photo. Sunset. Mom and dad young and laughing. My brothers playing. Me tickling Elizabeth's tiny, pudgy feet after burying her in the sand. Her giggles like all little kids, are filled up and bursting with joy. Just giggling and wiggling her toes.

I exhale. Blink to find Scarlett watching me. I close my eyes and run a hand through my hair, looking away from her eyes.

"I think you shouldn't waste your time fantasizing about things that can't be," I tell her just as we pull into the town and I see the chapel. Before she can open her mouth to reply, the SUV pulls to a stop and I climb out. I close the door behind me and take a deep breath in, grateful for the cooler temperature.

Charlie comes toward me. "Cristiano." We shake hands. "I finally get to meet your bride."

"Thanks for coming." Charlie will stand as my witness since Dante refused. He doesn't agree with the wedding in the church. He understands the necessity of it but won't accept the rest.

Incense hangs heavy in the fresh salty air.

I walk around to Scarlett's side and open her door.

She ignores my hand and slides out on her own. She looks around quickly but her eyes land on Charlie who smiles wide at her.

"I see why you've kept her locked away," he says.

She gives me the side-eye and I have to wonder at his choice of words.

"Charlie, this is my fiancée, Scarlett De La Cruz. Scarlett, Charlie Lombardi. Family friend and my right-hand man."

She looks at him again, shifts her gaze to his

outstretched hand. She reluctantly slips her hand into it but only momentarily.

"Very nice to meet you, Scarlett," Charlie says. "An honor to bear witness to your wedding."

She just studies him in silence, and I can almost hear the things she's telling him on the inside.

"Christ," I mutter.

Charlie just gives me a wink. "I'll see you at the altar."

Her gaze follows him to the chapel door where he disappears inside.

It's a small wooden structure and doesn't look like much from the outside. Our small group makes their way to the doors, Scarlett and I at the back, Noah near us. No one speaks.

Once there, Antonio opens the door. The place has been secured already. Even though no one knows we're here as opposed to the very public charity event, I'm not taking any chances.

My uncle thought we'd be married at the church in Naples where my parents had their ceremony. He sounded a little bitter when I wouldn't give him the details of our plans but seemed to accept it when I told him I didn't want to marry her in the same place my parents had been married. He doesn't know Charlie was invited.

This chapel, though, it's where my mom was baptized.

Rain begins to fall lightly. Scarlett and I are the

last to enter, leaving several soldiers outside. Once we're in the vestibule, I tell Noah to wait inside the church and turn to my bride-to-be.

She's looking at me, shivering a little. Raindrops dot her cheeks and two have fallen on her pretty, upturned nose. I wipe them off then brush her hands away from the coat in order to unbutton it and slip it off her shoulders. It's then I realize why she's been holding it closed all this time.

"Really, Scarlett?" I ask, shaking my head.

"I thought black was more fitting."

She's wearing a black dress appropriate for a funeral not a wedding.

I adjust the lace collar which has fallen over and use it to tug her closer, taking in her paler complexion, her wide eyes as she waits for my reaction.

"You're right," I start, playing her game. Winning it. "Black is more fitting for a cartel princess become mafia queen." I cup the back of her head, weave my fingers into her hair and tug when she pushes against my chest.

"I'm not your queen," she says.

"Not yet, but before the night is out, you will be mine. All mine."

Her expression turns into one of worry as she searches my eyes.

"Let's go get married," I tell her and shift my grip to her arm, bypassing her brother to walk her to the altar myself.

29

SCARLETT

Cristiano marches me down the aisle much the same way as he marched me upstairs last night.

The priest clears his throat, his smile vanishing when he sees the dress, sees Cristiano's hand around my arm.

The chapel is simple, the pews unadorned, the floors stone, some broken. If there are graves beneath them, they're so old their names and dates have been worn away by time. The altar though, is something to see. Arched ceilings painted turquoise, like the ocean. I bet during the day when sunlight shines through the stained-glass window, it's spectacular. The altar itself is as simply made as the pews but the gold chalice and the other paraphernalia are as beautiful as in any church. I wonder if they lock the gold away at night. I would.

But then again, I don't trust anyone.

"Begin," Cristiano commands, shifting his grip from my arm to my hand, weaving his fingers with mine. Not quite how lovers would hold hands but, holding on to me to let me know he has me. That I'm already his.

I'm sure he's not afraid I'll run off. I know what he'll do to Noah if I try anything.

So, I listen to the priest perform the ceremony in English. I guess I'm supposed to be grateful. I do speak enough Italian to follow but I haven't told him that.

When it's time for me to say the magic words, I do it with a glare into Cristiano's electric blue eyes. He just stares back at me, one corner of his mouth curving upward. He's entertained by me. I guess he's entertained is better than pissed off. I thought he'd already be angry about the dress but he's taking it in stride. Maybe he's choosing his battles. That's a win for me isn't it?

When it's his turn, he repeats the same vows I just took, minus the part about obeying. It's now time for the rings.

The priest prays over them before Cristiano slips mine onto my finger. It matches the engagement ring. He hands me a band to slide onto his finger. I'm tempted to toss it at him, but he must read my mind because he leans toward me and whispers, "Try me."

I don't.

I won't gamble with Noah's life. Just my own.

We're pronounced husband and wife and Cristiano is invited to kiss his bride. Not by said bride but by the priest.

I stand still and try not to feel anything. Try not to remember how it was last night. Try to ignore the flutter in my belly, the missed beat of my heart. Try not to taste him. Try really hard not to want to kiss him back because I like kissing Cristiano Grigori and I hate myself for it.

When he draws back, he brings his cheek to mine, mouth to my ear. "I can't wait to feel your lips wrapped around my cock tonight."

"I can't wait to bite your dick off," I whisper back enthusiastically.

He's smiling wide when he pulls away. Then wraps his hand around the back of my neck, big hand holding me possessively as we make our way down the aisle. Outside the church, Cristiano lifts me into one of the SUVs.

I think he's coming with me, but I'm surprised when he calls Alec over.

"Make sure you post a guard outside my wife's door," he says, eyes on me. "No one goes in and she definitely doesn't go out."

"Yes, sir."

"Where's my brother going?" I ask as he climbs into the same SUV as Lenore.

"Back to the island."

"But—"

"But nothing. He was at the wedding, as promised. He didn't walk you down the aisle because of your dress choice. I don't ask much but what I ask, I expect to be obeyed."

"You don't ask much? Are you even being serious?"

"As a bullet—"

"I got it," I cut him off, sit back and fold my arms across my chest.

With that, we're gone before I can even ask where he's going. Not that I care. I just want to know what's going on. Where I'm going to be while Noah returns to the island.

WE DRIVE FOR AN HOUR AND BY THE TIME WE ARRIVE at the beachfront house, it's completely dark and raining. The last mile or two were along a single lane road without any lamps. Guards were already stationed along the route.

I don't see any other SUVs and when I ask where we are exactly, I'm just ignored.

The house itself is pretty, simple but well-guarded. Although it doesn't feel like the fortress that is the island house. I'm escorted inside, taken through the living room and barely given a chance to look around before I'm led into what I guess is the master bedroom.

The room is large and decorated differently than the rest of the house. It has a decidedly softer style with fresh flowers everywhere, the king size bed scattered with rose petals which I promptly sweep off.

We're not lovers. We're not friends. We don't even like each other.

I go into the bathroom and find a large, free-standing tub, and a separate shower with a small window at the far end. Too small to crawl out of. At the pedestal sink I wash my face and look down at my rings.

I'm married.

Married to Cristiano Grigori.

The sound of someone opening the bedroom door has me switching off the water and steeling my spine. But when I return, I find a woman laying a table for dinner. Just one place setting. The guard watches her as she does, and no one pays any attention to me.

Once she's gone, I get to the table to find a plate of whole grilled fish, potatoes and roasted vegetables. There's also a small carafe of white wine with barely a glass of liquid inside. A folded note is propped against it.

I pick it up, open it.

Just to be sure you'll be up to feel every inch of me tonight.

"Jerk." It's because the first night I'd drunk myself to the point of passing out. I guess he's not taking any chances.

I only mean to eat a few bites of the food because I haven't eaten all day but end up finishing the plate and the tiny bit of wine.

Then, I wait.

30

CRISTIANO

I need to make one stop before going to my wife.

Jacob De La Cruz has just been discharged from the hospital. When I arrive at his home, he seems surprised. I don't think he realized I knew where he lived but he's quick to check his expression and invite me into the plain, uncared for house.

"You rent it furnished?" I ask although I already know.

"Easier," he says. "Whiskey?" he seems chastened. At least a little. His arm is in a sling, but it's not broken. He's got a soft bandage around it.

"How is it?" I gesture to it.

"Hurts when I move anything. But I have good meds."

He's not taking them though. I can tell from how tightly his face is set.

I take the whiskey he offers and drink a sip only because he drinks from his first and it was poured from the same bottle.

"So. Rinaldi was in Mexico all along?" he asks.

I nod.

"Didn't your uncle or someone in your organization have intelligence on him?"

"I'm not here to discuss my uncle or our organization, or even Rinaldi for that matter. I want you to arrange a meeting with Felix."

"Felix? I can communicate on your behalf."

"In person. Me and him. He's running the show down there, isn't that right?"

"We both are—"

"Except that they just shot you."

"That was an accident."

"Arrange a meeting." I shift my glass to my left hand and take a drink.

Jacob eyes the ring.

"Tell him Scarlett De La Cruz is Scarlett Grigori now."

"When did that happen?"

"Arrange it on neutral territory. Miami. In the next three days."

"Of course, Cristiano."

"Oh, and if Rinaldi should disappear, let your son-in-law know I'll take his head in the place of Rinaldi's."

He pales a little.

"And when I'm finished with Felix, I'll come after you." I finish my whiskey and put the glass down. "Let me know when you've talked to him."

I'm fucking done here.

31

CRISTIANO

lec greets me at the front door of the house. It's a small house on a large piece of property rarely used but maintained all the same. Neither the deed to the land nor the house are linked to my family. At least not unless you do some significant digging. Only a handful of people know of its existence, my brother, Charlie, Lenore, and the few soldiers I use when I'm here. Even my uncle doesn't know. It's a safe house in so far as the secrecy of its existence. I've been here a few times on my own in the last couple of years. It would drive my uncle crazy not knowing where I disappeared to but it's one of the things I've kept to myself, needing to.

As far as anyone knows, Scarlett and I went back to the island with everyone else.

"All quiet?" I ask Alec as I slip off my jacket and loosen my tie.

"For miles around." Access to the house is via a single road which can be surveilled easily. We have men stationed at checkpoints for three miles out.

"Good. And Scarlett?"

"Also quiet."

I nod, walk toward the large bedroom picking up the bottle of whiskey from the side table. The room takes up the back half of the house. Opening one of the double doors, I enter to find Scarlett standing at the window. Probably just figured out that it's locked because she's looking as irritated as ever.

My wife.

I smile. I like the sound of that. And I like her like this. Pissed off. It fits.

"It's locked," I say. Closing the door behind me, I set the bottle down and undo my tie.

"I figured that out."

"Were you going to climb out and run away?"

"Is Noah okay?" she asks, not bothering to answer my question, probably realizing how ridiculous it would have been to try and run.

"He's fine." I toss my tie aside and undo my cuffs, then the buttons of my shirt. I watch her as I strip it off. I walk over to the table and am pleased to see she's eaten. "Hunger strike over?"

"I wasn't on a hunger strike. I told you that. Nice note by the way. Very romantic."

I walk over to her, brush hair back from her face. "Is that what you want? Romance?"

"No." She pushes my hand away and tucks her hair behind her ears. For all her attitude, what I see in her eyes isn't quite fear. She's anxious. "Not from you."

"Who from then?" I feel myself tense.

"No one. Never mind." She tries to walk past me, but I block her path.

"Who?"

"I said no one. Who would there be, Cristiano? I haven't exactly had the opportunity to date."

I step closer, backing her up to the wall. I set my forearms on either side of her head. Our bodies touching, chest to chest. I can see her pulse throb fast at her neck. She's barefoot and has to crane her neck to look up at me.

"I like you in black. It fits your usual mood." I lean my face down, kiss her. Just a quick kiss. A claiming of her lower lip.

Her teeth snap. "You make my mood black."

"Be nice," I say, wiping the drop of blood from my lip. "I'm about to make you come." I kiss her again. She's not kissing me back exactly, but her mouth is open. When I sweep my tongue across hers, she gasps. Her small hands curl around my shoulders before pushing me away as if she just remembered she should.

I draw back just a little, keeping her caged and our bodies pressed together, my cock rigid between us. "Speaking of, do you know you called me god when I ate your pussy last night?"

Her cheeks flush and she shoves me again. This time I let her slip past.

I pour myself a whiskey as I watch her open the door, see the men just outside our bedroom, and promptly close it again. I take a sip, give her a few minutes to wrap her brain around what comes next as her gaze bounces around the room. A trapped bird.

No, a trapped little kitten whose razor-sharp claws I need to look out for.

She finally stops, faces me.

"Strip, Scarlett."

She narrows her eyes. "Make me, Cristiano."

I swallow and set the glass aside. "Gladly."

She yelps when I stalk toward her and I wonder what she expected. Me to back down? Or a war of words. She's more than capable of that, I know, but that's not what I want. Not tonight. Not on my wedding night.

I grasp her arms, sliding my hands to her wrists as I walk her back to the bed. Our bodies are touching, eyes never once leaving one another's.

Switching my grip so both wrists are in one hand, I take hold of the zipper at the back of the dress and slide it down slowly. I let my fingers brush the bare skin of her back as they move, feeling imaginary sparks. I watch her pupils dilate and hear her breath hitch.

She doesn't say a word as I release her wrists and push the dress off her shoulders. It slips to the floor so she's standing in a black lace bra and panties. I draw back just a little to look at her before stepping backward. I cross the room to pour another whiskey and take a seat on the armchair setting one ankle over the opposite knee.

"Take off the rest."

She swallows, glances around again. There's no escape. She knows that.

For a long moment I just watch her as she battles herself, see an array of emotions pass through her. The most prominent being rage. Eventually she reaches back and unhooks her bra, no slow strip tease for me. Nothing erotic at all as she strips off the rest of her things, stumbling as she tries to step out of her panties before walking toward me, standing just inches from me.

"Is this what you want?" She glances down at my crotch then drags her gaze back up to mine. "You hard for it, Cristiano?"

I let my gaze slide over her naked body, take in the lines of slender, toned muscle, small breasts barely a handful, the neat little triangle of dark hair. I'm slow to return my gaze to hers.

"I am, Little Kitten. I've never been this hard for a woman before."

"I'm flattered," she deadpans.

I finish my drink, setting the glass down and standing before her. I don't even have to touch her to walk her back to the bed, my chest brushing hers.

When the backs of her knees hit the bed, her legs bend but she rights herself, standing tall, nipples poking against my chest.

"Now turn around, bend over and spread your legs wide so I can decide which hole I'm fucking first."

Her hands slap my chest. "Fuck you!"

"That's my girl." I grab hold of her wrists and spin her around, breathe in her scent at her neck where her pulse throbs.

"You'll bend to me, Little Kitten." I bite the curve of her neck.

"You'll have to make me."

"With pleasure."

I lean over her, pushing her torso down. Keeping her wrists at her lower back, I straighten and use my knee to widen her stance.

She goes still as I take her in, her beautiful ass open to me. My dick is a fucking steel rod.

When I touch her hip, she jumps like she wasn't expecting it. She's up on tiptoe, lean calf and hamstring muscles tensing.

"Stay," I tell her. I let go of her wrists. She remarkably does as she's told.

Hands on her cheeks, I splay her open, look at her. At her tiny asshole, the open lips of her pussy.

She tries to clench her cheeks, but I keep her open.

"You're so fucking beautiful like this. Your pussy open and wet for me. Your asshole so tempting." I touch my thumb to her asshole and she clenches.

"Cristiano—"

But her breath catches as I crouch down and extend the tip of my tongue to her clit and lick all the way up through her wet folds to her other hole, laying the flat of my tongue on her as I repeat downward then back again, tasting her, wanting her. Wanting every fucking part of her.

"Oh god," she whimpers, and I draw back to watch a slow trickle of arousal slide down her inner thigh.

"Fucking perfect," I tell her, standing. "Stay."

She does and turns just her head to watch me strip off the rest of my clothes. She licks her lips when I take my cock into my hand and run it through her folds. Her eyes close as I smear her wetness over myself.

"So fucking perfect." I lean down for one more taste before tugging her to stand, spinning her to face me and kissing her hard.

She doesn't bite but I wouldn't care if she did right now. I want this. And she wants this. And neither of us can deny it.

I lay her on the bed, holding my weight on my elbows as I draw back to look at her. My cock is nestled against her wet cunt.

Her eyes have gone dark. I kiss her again, put my hands on her inner thighs to open her wider and when I draw back to look at her, I see a tear.

It sobers me.

She's probably scared. Doesn't quite know what to expect.

"I'm not going to hurt you, Scarlett."

"It's not...I just don't understand why I want this," she admits, another tear sliding down her temple.

I smile to her, kiss her. She kisses me back.

Drawing back, I place a hand on her chest to keep her lying back, using the other to keep one leg spread wide. She doesn't try to close her legs, however. From here, I can see she's slick and in spite of her fear, I smell her arousal.

I need to make her come before I take her. It'll be easier for her.

I dip my head and hear her gasp when I close my mouth over her. Twirling my tongue in a circle around the hard little nub before sucking, I open my mouth wide to take the whole of her, tickling her other hole before returning my attention to her clit.

She gasps my name, her hands to my head, fingers pulling my hair.

"Come, Scarlett. Let me feel you come."

It doesn't take long for her to come and I drink it in, the taste of her intoxicating as she calls out my name in a long string. She's just repeating, repeating, repeating, making my dick throb as if it's confused why it's not inside her. Only when her legs relax do I straighten and meet her eyes, a soft caramel now.

She's so fucking beautiful. So perfect.

I lift her higher on the bed, settle between her legs, my cock at her entrance. I kiss her again, realizing she's kissing me back, and I don't think I can get enough of her.

When she feels me at her entrance she tenses.

"I won't hurt you," I mutter against her mouth but I'm not sure I'll be able to help it. Her first time will hurt.

I take her hands in mine, weave my fingers with hers and I push in a little farther. The effort of holding back is taking every ounce of energy I have. I need to take care with her, though. I move slowly, in and out, inch by inch when the animal inside me wants to thrust hard, wants to feel her resistance and rip through it, feel the warm rush of virgin blood.

She's tight. I swear she's tighter than any woman I've been with, but it's been a long time, so what do I know. And when she begins panting again, her passage slick, I know she's ready.

I hold onto her, want to give her something to hold on to. I push deeper, still controlled, expecting resistance, expecting blood.

There's a moment suspended. Something not right.

Because it doesn't come.

The fact registers slowly. I pump in and out twice more then stop.

She makes a sound when I do and opens her eyes to meet mine, forehead wrinkled in disappointment.

"You're not a virgin."

I can hardly process the silence.

"You're not—"

"I never said I was."

I think back and she's right. She didn't. I assumed it.

I blink, pull out. I'm still hard. I look down at myself, still searching for evidence to the contrary of what I know is true. But there's nothing there. No blood.

"You let me believe it."

I walk away, run a hand through my hair not sure why I care. Why it matters.

No. I know why.

She's right. She never said she was. But she didn't correct me either. And it feels like a betrayal. Because after everything, I was still counting on her. On one person I could trust.

"You let me believe it," I say again, turning to find her sitting up on the bed. "You fucking let me believe it." *Let me believe in you.*

"I didn't lie to you. You assumed—"

"Omission is a lie. You're a liar."

She pulls her knees up, wraps her arms around them, her face falling. "I'm not—"

"Just like your brothers," I add, distaste marking my words.

"What?" Her forehead wrinkles and I register hurt in her eyes.

"I don't know why I thought you were different." I pull on my briefs, my pants.

"I—"

"You shook your ass, and I was just hard up enough to notice." I grab my shirt.

"I didn't. I never—"

I spin to face her, my arm poised to slap her.

She gasps, shielding herself as she cowers, and I realize what I was about to do.

I make a fist. It's all I can do with the rage I feel, but let it drop to my side while she watches me, eyes wide, face partially hidden by her arms.

Muttering a curse, I walk away.

"Cristiano, I—"

I look at her again but keep my distance. "You're a liar, Scarlett! A fucking liar!"

"I..." She looks stunned and afraid, her cheeks wet with tears. But I won't let those fool me. I remember how just hours ago, she told me in no uncertain terms that we are enemies. When I confided in her and told her I needed a friend. Just one. When I asked her to be that friend, she refused me.

And I was a fucking idiot not to take that at face value. This is my fault. I brought this on myself.

"Don't cry. Don't you dare fucking cry." I button up my shirt and tuck it into my pants.

"I didn't lie to you! I never lied to you!"

"Were you having a good laugh? Huh? A good laugh at my expense? You fucked him, didn't you? You fucked Marcus Rinaldi?"

"No. God. Never." She's outright crying now, hugging herself tightly, shivering.

"Did you like it? Did you come for him? Call out his name like you do mine?"

She just shakes her head, the skin around her eyes puffy and pink, tears streaming.

"And I felt sorry for you when I found out what your brothers had done to you. How they'd humiliated you. But you probably liked it."

She just stares at me with those damn tears coming like a fucking waterfall, big eyes looking like she can't quite believe what's happening.

She's been caught. That's what's happening.

I pick up the bottle of whiskey, drink a swallow.

I gave her my mother's ring. Like a fucking idiot, I put my mother's ring on this whore's finger.

Christ. What the fuck is wrong with me?

Rage like nothing I've felt before consumes me.

With a roar, I throw the bottle across the room and watch it smash against the wall.

Scarlett screams and leaps off the bed to run toward the bathroom.

I stalk her and before she can get there, catch her by her hair and tug her backward, tossing her face-down on the bed. She's up in an instant, scrambling on her hands and knees across the bed, but I grab an ankle and tug her back to me.

She drops onto her stomach. I pull her toward me smacking her ass hard enough to make her scream again.

"I didn't lie—"

I flip her onto her back, straddle her. She's still crying.

"Shut up. Shut the fuck up, you fucking whore."

"Cris—"

I grip her jaw, cutting off her words. I squeeze but it only makes her cry harder. She tries to pull her arms free, but I've got them trapped at her sides. I can only look down at her, at my fingers bruising her jaw, at her eyes big as saucers.

"I can break you. Snap your neck. Do you know how easy it would be?"

She whimpers, tears streaming from the corners of both eyes onto the bed.

"I should. If I were smart, I would."

"Please," she manages.

"I'm an idiot, aren't I?" I let go of her jaw, drag her

left arm free, look at the ring. I betrayed my family for her. For this woman who made me remember and somehow gave me hope. Fucking hope.

This woman, who I have to remember is my enemy.

"You said you wouldn't hurt me," she says.

I shift my gaze to her eyes, and I see fear.

"That was before. I warned you what would happen if you betrayed me."

I return my attention to her hand, drag both rings off her finger, pocket the engagement ring and leave the other one on the bed. I slide off of her, look at her lying there, looking into her eyes again. As she rubs her finger where the rings were, the tears keep streaming down her cheeks.

"You wanted an enemy, Scarlett. I'll remember it from now on."

32

SCARLETT

I hear the lock turn a moment after he's gone.

My heart is racing and I'm shivering. He was so angry. But I never lied to him. There just wasn't any way I could tell him.

Whore.

The word rings like an accusation. It's not the first time I've been called one but this time, hearing it from him, it hurts.

He accused me of fucking Marcus Rinaldi. If I had, it wouldn't have been consensual. Doesn't he know that? I'm not a whore.

And I don't know why I'm sitting here crying. I should be pissed. Offended.

Or relieved. He won't touch me again. It's what I wanted, isn't it? We're enemies now, truly. It's what I told him I wanted.

I shiver with cold as the rain outside beats down

on the house. I pull the blanket up around my shoulders and the wedding band drops to the tiled floor. It bounces once before coming to rest.

I feel sad. So fucking sad. I feel like I did at the house after he told me about his enemies and asked me to be his friend.

Maybe he's right. Maybe I am just like my brothers. I should have told him when he assumed I was a virgin. I should have said something. But what? I couldn't. I still wouldn't.

I hear a car engine outside and go to the window. Two SUVs are driving too fast in this rain. He's leaving? Just driving away?

I rub my face, shudder again, the cold settling deeper inside me.

He asked me to be his friend. His one friend. What about his brother or his uncle? Aren't they at least his allies? Or are they enemies too?

I'm not paying attention as I walk back to the bed and wince when I step on a shard of glass from the whiskey bottle. It cuts into my foot, leaving a trace of red on the tile.

I balance on one leg to pull the glass out and drop it to the floor.

Gingerly, I walk into the bathroom and close the door. Sitting on the edge of the tub, I check to make sure I haven't missed any more glass. When I sit, still feeling him inside me. Sticky between my legs from when he made me come.

I turn on the water, test the temperature, then plug the drain. I wish he hadn't broken that bottle of whiskey. I'd have happily downed it now. Instead, I slip into the tub and listen to the sound of the water eat up the silence. And as the weight of what just happened settles alongside the cold in my belly, I shudder, adjusting the water temperature so on any other day, it would be too hot to stand.

It takes a long time to fill the tub. Not that it matters. It's not like I have plans. Cristiano is gone. I'm sure he's left a slew of soldiers to make sure I stay put. Not that it would take a slew.

He just needs to calm down and when he comes back, I'll explain. I'll make something up. A biking accident when I was little. Don't girls lose their virginity that way? Or is that just an old wives' tale? I can't tell him the truth. I won't. I will never tell him that truth.

I shake my head, reach to switch off the water. I lay my head back and let myself cry. I'm not even sure why I care. Why it bothers me even a little what he thinks of me. Because isn't he my enemy? Isn't that what I swore to him and to myself?

33

CRISTIANO

The stripper dancing on stage is a blur of movement because all I see is red.

Scarlett isn't a virgin.

She's supposed to be a virgin. And why the fuck this bothers me, I have no clue.

Tilting the bottle back I drink a swig of whiskey. It's almost empty. I get up from my seat, but the moment I do, I feel hands on me.

I grip the back of the chair. Close my eyes in the hopes it'll make the room stop spinning.

Someone's talking and fuck, I'm drunk. I am so drunk.

"Jesus Christ," a man says. I open my eyes only to find my uncle shoving his way toward me. "What the hell, Cristiano?" He gestures to two of my men following him.

"I told you to wait outside," I tell them.

The soldiers stop. Look from me to my uncle.

I turn to my uncle. "Why are you here?"

"Get him in the car. This is embarrassing," he instructs the two men as he attempts to take my whiskey away.

"That's mine."

"Fine. Drink yourself to death. What do I care."

We're outside a moment later. Rain is coming down in sheets and I'm soaked by the time I'm in the SUV. My uncle climbs in beside me.

I blink, then widen my eyes. "I wasn't done in there."

"If you want a prostitute I'll get you one. A clean one." He shakes his head, shifts his gaze to his suit jacket, the disgust unmistakable. "I'm going to have to burn this suit."

"You need to lighten up, Uncle." I swig more of my whiskey.

"Is that from tonight?" He gestures to the bottle.

I look at it. Note how little liquid is left inside it. I nod.

"Christ." He shakes his head, glances at my ring finger. "What's the matter, Cristiano? Trouble in paradise? And on your wedding night?"

"None of your business," I say, suddenly remembering I'd put my mom's ring in my pocket. I feel for it and I'm relieved to find it's still there.

"It becomes my business when I get a call at two

in the morning telling me you're wasted in just about the seediest strip club in town."

I lay my head back against the seat. "I'm tired."

He sighs. "She's not worth getting upset over. Certainly not this upset."

"I said I'm tired."

"Fine. We'll talk in the morning when you're sober. I just hope this night straightens you out. You let that whore turn your head—"

My hand is around his throat in an instant. I'm not even sure how I move that fast, considering, but I'm squeezing, fuming.

"You do not call her that."

He sputters, one hand around my forearm, face reddening. The car comes to a screeching stop.

"You. Do. Not. Fucking. Call. Her. That."

I'm not sure which comes first then. The cocking of a pistol or the cold steel against my throat.

34

SCARLETT

I t's so quiet, it's almost eerie. I look up at the ceiling, watching steam rise from my bath. I hear a drop of water fall into the tub. That's it. That's the only sound. And it feels somehow wrong.

The bedroom door opens. I turn my head, but from this angle I can't see who it is. It's quiet again. Like whoever opened the door just walked away.

"Cristiano?" I ask quietly, sitting up, drawing my knees toward my chest.

He doesn't answer. No one does, but if I listen closely, I hear footsteps in the living room, then whispers. Men's whispers. Soldiers?

No.

Not soldiers.

Ice coats my spine when I hear his voice. He shouldn't be here. Cristiano wouldn't allow him to be here.

Would he? He wouldn't do that to me, would he?

I look around for a robe, a towel. Something to cover myself, but his footsteps become more pronounced. He's not trying to be quiet. The opposite.

He's in the bedroom so I remain in the tub, my arms hugging my knees to my chest.

And then he's leaning against the doorway. He cocks his head to the side. When I try to swallow, my throat closes up.

I don't want to show fear. But I am afraid.

If I'm honest, I've always been afraid of him. I just lied to myself when I said I wasn't, because sometimes you need to lie to yourself to survive.

"Scarlett," he says, walking into the bathroom, eyes roaming my body. He sits on the edge of the tub and extends the arm that's not in the sling into the water, fingers skimming it, not touching me but creating a ripple. "Where's your groom?"

Relief. Cristiano didn't send him. But that relief is short-lived.

"He'll be right back," I say.

"Hm. I don't think he will." His gaze moves to my breasts, which are fairly well hidden by my legs. He tilts his head, touching my knee. I resist, water splashing as he pries a knee open to have a good look.

"I thought you only liked little girls, Uncle."

He drags his gaze over my body and up to meet mine. "Oh, I'm not looking for myself."

It takes all I have not to physically shake at his words. I hold his gaze, even though all I can see is him over me, on top of me. All I feel is sweat dripping on me as he grunts. All I feel is him inside me. Hurting me.

God. I'm going to be sick.

"But you'll still bring in some money. Cartel Princess on the auction block. Do you know how many enemies your brothers made? Just imagine the ways they can punish you for their wrongs."

"Where's Cristiano? What did you do to him?"

He stands up, shakes off his hand and gestures to the two soldiers who come into view. I don't recognize them.

"Get up."

"Fuck you."

"Lift her out."

They're on either side of me before I can make a move. Two sets of hands hauling me to my feet, water dripping off me, splashing onto the bathroom floor as I fight. It's no use, I know.

"Where's Cristiano?" I yell to my uncle as he stands perusing me.

"Take her."

One of the soldiers reaches for a towel.

"Like she is," my uncle instructs, and the soldier

only hesitates momentarily before he drops the towel.

I fight as they lift me off my feet, kicking when they throw me face down onto the bed and drag my arms behind my back. Binding my wrists first, then my ankles. I manage to kick one in the nose before they can secure my legs.

Once I'm bound, they stand me up. The one I kicked wasn't the one who had reached for the towel. He raises an arm to slap me, but my uncle grabs it.

"Not her face," he says. "Don't mess up her face."

But when the soldier makes a fist to punch me in my belly, he doesn't interfere. He just looks on as I double over, the wind knocked out of me so I can't even scream.

Once is enough, but he does it a second time, before I'm lifted, doubled over, and carried out through the house. I see Alec on the floor at the opposite end of the room. He's cradling his arm but he's alive. The rest of Cristiano's soldiers are lying on the ground dead or dying. I wonder how I didn't hear the bullets, but I know a moment later when we get outside. Another soldier is dragged to his knees and executed with a bullet to the back of the head. The gun is fitted with a silencer.

I'd scream but this isn't the first time I've seen this. Not even the second or third. And it all happens so fast. The icy rain on my naked skin, my feet scraping against stone, shin slammed into the back of the car as I kick my legs, bound to make a mermaid's tail. I'm lifted and dumped into the trunk of a waiting car.

CRISTIANO

I t's a dream. I know it. There's a texture to it. An echo in the sound. I know it and it still doesn't make a difference. This fucking nightmare, this chapter of my life, will always own me.

Except that this time, something's different. But I can't figure out what it is.

The marble is cold beneath me as I watch the blood circle widen. Deep red on pristine white.

They're already here. My brothers. My father. I can hear them, but I can't open my eyes to see.

I hear her too. My mother.

I drag my eyelids open. The first thing I see is my own reflection in the mirror of blood. My face white as the marble should be.

I should have died. Why didn't I die?

They're on their knees. Michael's already dead. His eyes are open but he's already dead.

That echo comes again and then I hear it. I hear him tear her dress. See her pushed to her knees in my periphery. See her hands slip in Michael's blood.

She's wearing a red dress tonight. She wasn't wearing red that night. But maybe that's blood on the dress and I can't see straight.

I want to wake up. I want to wake the fuck up. Too much whiskey. My uncle was right.

"I figure if I'm drunk enough, it won't hurt as much."

No. That's wrong. That's Scarlett's voice. She doesn't belong here. Not in this dream.

But she's here and she's crying. Sobbing. Calling for me. Asking for help. Pleading for it.

And I can't move. But when I open my eyes again, I see him. I see Marcus on her and all I can do is lie there in my own blood. All I can do is watch him do it just like the last time.

"...won't hurt as much."

But it's not my mother on her knees before him. It's not her in the red dress.

I claw at the floor, hands slipping in my own blood. And she's calling for me. She's begging me to help her. To make him stop. And I can't fucking get to her.

"...won't hurt as much."

He hurt her. That's why she'd drank so much the first night because she expected pain. I remember it now.

I wouldn't have hurt her.

"Scarlett." Does she hear me? "I'm coming."

But I'm not. I can't. All I can do is watch her face lying in Michael's blood. Tears streaming from her eyes as Marcus moves behind her. Until the end. Until the very end when he brings the knife to her throat and whispers something I can't hear. Something that makes her mouth fall open as he grins like Satan himself and slides the knife across her throat. And I swear I hear it. I hear the ripping of skin. Hear the pouring of blood.

"No!"

I jolt upright and the moment I do, it's like I rammed my head into a fucking brick wall.

"Fuck."

I look around. Remember.

After I left the house, I went to a strip club. I don't even know why. I'm not even a little interested in those women. And then there was whiskey. A lot of whiskey before someone called my uncle and he came. I tried to strangle him when he called Scarlett a whore. He pulled a gun on me.

Which explains why I'm in my room at the Naples house with a fucking pounding headache. I'm actually not sure if I'm hungover or still drunk.

I get up and have to hold on while the world rights itself.

"I figure if I'm drunk enough, it won't hurt as much."

I get to the bathroom, take a piss then wash my

hands and my face. I look like hell. Like death barely warmed over. I'm surprised the mirror doesn't crack.

"I figure if I'm drunk enough, it won't hurt as much."

Scarlett's voice repeats that sentence for the tenth fucking time. I remember when she said it. How I thought it sounded odd. And I think about last night. About how I felt when I was inside her. When I realized the truth.

Betrayed. That's the feeling. It hardens you.

"I figure if I'm drunk enough, it won't hurt as much."

I open the medicine cabinet and swallow four aspirin. It won't help, I already know.

I'm just walking out of the bathroom when the bedroom door opens. My uncle is standing there with a strange look on his face. He's not dressed in his usual suit but in his pajamas. I'm not sure I've seen him in anything but a suit since I was a kid.

"What time is it?"

"Early. Seven."

I glance to the window. The sun is a line of deep orange in the break of dark clouds that still dirty the sky. I turn back to my uncle, sobering up as I take in the pajamas, the expression on his face.

Warning bells ring in my ears. Something is wrong. Something is very wrong.

"What is it? What's happened?" I hear myself ask.

"There was a problem."

My heart races as my brain processes. "What problem?"

"You should have told me where you were going."

"What. Problem."

"Sit down."

"Fucking tell me."

"There was an ambush."

"What?" My stomach bottoms out.

"All the soldiers are dead."

Dead. "Scarlett?"

"They were probably looking for you."

"Scarlett?" I ask again through gritted teeth.

"It's a good thing you weren't there."

"Scarlett!" I demand.

"Gone."

We drive for hours. Or at least it feels like hours. All I hear in the trunk of this old, beat up sedan is rain. All I feel is every bump, every tiny stone, every pothole on the road.

My wrists are bound behind my back. My shoulders and arms ache and the zip ties they bound me with cut into the skin of my wrists. I've managed to turn myself, so my feet touch one of the rear lights. I'm not sure what I hope to accomplish though. Kicking out the light? And then what?

After a sharp, bumpy turn and a long road of what must be gravel, the car slows to a stop. My heartbeat picks up. I hadn't realized it had calmed at all during the drive. I hear men outside, smell cigarette smoke. They're speaking Spanish. That's the one thing of importance to note. Cartel soldiers?

Makes sense. Most important question is what am I to them? Their enemy's wife or the cartel's princess?

I'm going to guess the former since I'm riding naked in the trunk.

Someone pops the trunk and although dawn has hardly broken, I have to squint after the complete darkness of the trunk. I hear seagulls overhead and smell fish. As I start to move, the man who punched me, reaches in to lift me out.

We've arrived at a harbor. A crappy, run-down little harbor nothing like the ones tourists go to. The boats at the docks look like they had their best days a century ago.

I smell dead fish and cigarette smoke as I stand shivering in the cold morning air, my feet bare on the gravel, my body naked.

Someone lights a match, and my attention is drawn to the sound. It's my uncle.

Without a glance, he walks past me toward another man I don't know. That man gestures with a nod and my uncle walks to a sedan with tinted windows. It's parked just beyond a busted streetlamp in the shadow of a building. I can just make out the shape of two heads in the backseat.

The door opens and I see a pair of khaki slacks. I squint my eyes to see who it is and my heart pounds, the alarm in my head sounding the warning to run. The man inside places a hand on the car door to help himself out. The watch. I know it. And I feel the blood drain from my face as Marcus Rinaldi steps out of the vehicle. Both he and my uncle turn to me.

I make a sound and I realize when my body tries to move, to run, that I'm still bound at ankles and wrists while two soldiers hold me still.

From here I see Marcus's gaze slide over me, watch his grin widen as he takes me in.

The hands tighten on my arms as I draw back.

Stealing my attention, I notice another man leering at me. This one bigger, with stains on the belly of his shirt, lazily walking toward us. I have no reason to think Marcus or my uncle will protect me if any of these other men try to touch me. The opposite.

The man looks me over; places the cigarette he's smoking between his lips and reaches behind him. When he pulls out a hunting knife, I open my mouth to scream or beg. But he bends down to cut the zip ties at my ankles then puts the knife away.

The sound of a truck engine has us all turning to the lone road that we must have traveled to come to this decrepit place. We watch as the truck pulls up. It's beat up and the logo on the side too faded for me to read. But it doesn't matter because when it comes to a stop and the container door is lifted, I see them, realizing what this is. I finally realize what's about to happen. It makes me fight again, twist against the two soldiers holding me. We all watch, including my uncle and Marcus.

The other man in the car is still a mystery. I can still see the outline of his head from here.

We just stand there and watch the women and girls lifted off the truck. I count a dozen. All in various states of dress, some with bound wrists. All looking terrified as they're led single file down to the waiting boat which has just started its engine.

One tries to run and a soldier punches her. Just punches her right in the temple. The force of it knocks her sideways. Someone else screams as she staggers, stumbles, tries again to run. The soldier doesn't punch her this time. He takes his gun out, cocks it, and shoots her in the stomach.

I don't scream but the others do. In my periphery, I see my uncle take a drag off his cigarette while Marcus watches the scene with cold indifference.

The woman drops to the ground and the others behind her are made to step over her body. She's still alive, curled around herself, clutching her stomach. Blood expands in a circle around her, as the man who pulled the trigger, nudges her with his foot and then laughs.

She'll bleed to death. And it will be excruciatingly painful.

That's when I hear my name.

I turn to find my uncle and Marcus walking toward me. My uncle is talking, still casually smoking. I remember he used to smoke but had told my brothers he'd given it up.

Marcus puts his sunglasses on as the sunlight breaks the horizon. I stiffen when they approach, and I'm dragged forward to meet them.

"She's a little bit of a handful. You may remember," my uncle starts, but I'm too shocked to speak, too terrified to fight. Will I be loaded onto that boat too? Then what? What will happen? Will Cristiano find me? Will he bother to look for me? Will he know or even care what happened to me?

Behind them, the car door opening snags my attention. It's the other man from the backseat. But he's got his back to me so I can't see his face.

"You did good," Marcus tells my uncle, gaze lecherous, the licking of his lips turning my stomach.

Even as my shock at seeing him registers, there's more in store. It happens so fast. These things always happen so shockingly fast.

Marcus moves his arm behind him and then there's a click. Just a soft little click. I know my uncle hears it too because his grin falters as he begins to turn in the direction of Marcus. I wonder if he registers what is about to happen, as Marcus raises the gun, leveling it with my uncle's forehead.

There isn't any hesitation on Marcus's side. Nothing but that cool smile on his lips.

It all happens in the span of moments. Split seconds. The man from the car turns, the sun's shifting position not allowing me to see his face. He's just a shape at the far end of the lot.

My uncle's grinning expression morphs into one of terror.

Marcus pulls the trigger and for the third time in almost as many days, blood splatters across my face and into my mouth. My uncle's body falls sideways to the ground. Dead. Just like that. Dead, while the woman who was shot moments ago still moans in agony as her life slowly bleeds out of her.

Dead. Final. The end.

I look at Marcus, his eyes on my chest travel lower as he tucks the gun into the back of his khakis. An erection presses against the front of his pants. He's aroused. It's not from looking at me. It's from the kill. Violence always aroused him.

The other man from the car says something. He's speaking English, but with an accent. I still can't make out his face. The sun is blinding. But when Marcus steps toward me, my attention is fully on him as I try to free myself of the vise-like grips of the soldiers.

Marcus takes a syringe out of the breast pocket of his shirt and pushes the plunger, clearing any air.

"Long time no see," he says in that voice that always turned my blood to ice. Without warning, he grips a handful of my hair and forces my head to the side to push the needle into my neck.

I feel the effects almost instantly as my knees give out, touching gravel, the soldiers' hands still painful on my arms.

"Cover her for fuck's sake," the man with the accented English says and I feel something over my shoulders. I can almost place the aftershave, but my vision has faded. Voices, too, just sounds I can't make out. I'm dragged to where I hear the water lapping against the boats, hear the sounds of frightened women. Their warm bodies the last thing I feel against my own before I lose consciousness.

Thank you for reading **With This Ring**. I hope you enjoyed this first part of Cristiano and Scarlett's story. I truly loved writing it.

Their story concludes in *I Thee Take*, the second and final book of the *To Have and To Hold Duet* available in all stores!
One-Click I Thee Take now!

ALSO BY NATASHA KNIGHT

MacLeod Brothers

Devil's Bargain

Benedetti Mafia World

Salvatore: a Dark Mafia Romance

Dominic: a Dark Mafia Romance

Sergio: a Dark Mafia Romance

The Benedetti Brothers Box Set (Contains Salvatore, Dominic and Sergio)

Killian: a Dark Mafia Romance

Giovanni: a Dark Mafia Romance

The Amado Brothers

Dishonorable

Disgraced

Unhinged

Standalone Dark Romance

Descent

Deviant

Beautiful Liar

Retribution

Theirs To Take

Captive, Mine

Alpha

Given to the Savage

Taken by the Beast

Claimed by the Beast

Captive's Desire

Protective Custody

Amy's Strict Doctor

Taming Emma

Taming Megan

Taming Naia

Reclaiming Sophie

The Firefighter's Girl

Dangerous Defiance

Her Rogue Knight

Taught To Kneel

Tamed: the Roark Brothers Trilogy

THANK YOU!

Thanks for reading **With This Ring**. I hope you enjoyed it. Reviews help new readers find books and would make me ever grateful. Please consider leaving a review at the store where you purchased the book.

Click here to sign up for my newsletter to receive new release news and updates!

Like my FB Author Page to keep updated on news and giveaways!

I have a FB Fan Group where I share exclusive teasers, giveaways and just fun stuff. Probably TMI :) It's called The Knight Spot. I'd love for you to join us! Just click here!

ABOUT THE AUTHOR

Natasha Knight is the *USA Today* Bestselling author of Romantic Suspense and Dark Romance Novels. She has sold over half a million books and is translated into six languages. She currently lives in The Netherlands with her husband and two daughters and when she's not writing, she's walking in the woods listening to a book, sitting in a corner reading or off exploring the world as often as she can get away.

Write Natasha here: natasha@natasha-knight.com

Click here to sign up for my newsletter to receive new release news and updates!

NATASHA KNIGHT
sexy dark romance with heart

www.natasha-knight.com
natasha-knight@outlook.com

Printed in Great Britain
by Amazon

32650998R00192